DANCING SHOES

Dancing Shoes

Noel Streatfeild

Illustrated by Richard Floethe

A YEARLING BOOK

Published by
Dell Publishing Co., Inc.
1 Dag Hammarskjold Plaza
New York, New York 10017

Yearling ® TM 913705, Dell Publishing Co., Inc.

ISBN: 0-440-42289-2

Reprinted by arrangement with Random House, Inc.
Printed in the United States of America
Fourth Dell printing—August 1982
CW

CONTENTS

CONTENTS

DANCING SHOES

1

THE DANCING SCHOOL

The School of Dancing was in North London. Outside it looked just an ordinary house, rather big perhaps for the shabby neighborhood to which it belonged. But it was anything but ordinary to the neighbors, who knew that in it were trained Mrs. Wintle's Little Wonders.

Cora Wintle had danced on the stage. She had never got beyond the chorus, for though she danced well she did not have a good figure, nor was she pretty. But she had loved the life, and had found it hard to give it up when she had fallen in love and married an artist called Tom Lennox. Tom was a good painter, but a poor earner of money.

Tom and Cora had been married about a year when they had a baby. She was a little girl, and they christened her Dulcie. It was after Dulcie was born that Cora saw that if she was to bring the child up properly she must have more money than Tom was likely to earn. That was when she had her big idea. Why should she waste her dancing talent? She was getting old for chorus work and anyway she could not be away from home, but why should she not teach others to dance?

Cora was a person who usually by determination got her own way. If she had not been that type she would never have got into any chorus, for she was usually turned down at sight. But she had refused to be beaten, and had worn managements down by her persistence until they had said:

"Engage Cora Wintle. I'm tired of saying no."

The dancing school had its start two days after Cora had first thought of it. She was out shopping with Dulcie when by mistake she pushed the perambulator into a passer-by, a woman, not at all young but fat and cozy-looking. The woman won her way straight to Cora's heart by not being at all angry about the perambulator hitting her in the stomach, but instead being rapturous about Dulcie.

"Oh, what a little love," she said in a warm, purry voice. "I've looked after many a baby in my time, but I never saw a prettier."

That conversation led to a cup of tea in a shop. There is nothing like a cup of tea for telling things. In no time Cora was explaining about Tom not earning much, and her dream of a dancing school.

"I was well trained myself, and I would see any child that came to me was well trained. I shall call myself Wintle, as that's how I'm known in the theater. Tom won't mind."

The stranger, whose name was Miss Purser, then told Cora about herself.

"I've been a children's Nannie since I was a slip of a girl, but now, provided I can be with children, I might give it up. My ship's come in, so to speak, only I wish it hadn't the way it has. One of my babies, the Honorable George Point . . . maybe you read of it in the papers. Eaten by a shark he was."

"Goodness," said Cora, "a shark! Just fancy, and him an Honorable too."

Miss Purser shook her head.

"No respecter of persons, sharks aren't. Well, when

5

the will was read it was found he'd left his old Nan a little money and a house, bless him. In North London the house is, not a nice part, and a great barrack of a place."

The idea hit them both at the same moment. There was Miss Purser with a house suitable for a dancing school, and wanting to be with children, and there was Cora with the training to teach children to dance. Why should they not become partners?

A few months later Cora moved her family, and Miss Purser moved herself, into Miss Purser's house. Cora put an advertisement in the local paper.

"Cora Wintle, teacher of children for the stage. Classes daily. 67, Ford Road, Tel. PRImrose 15150."

She showed the advertisement to Miss Purser, whom by then she was calling Pursey.

"How's that, Pursey?"

"Very nice, Mrs. Wintle. Now I do wonder who your first pupil will be."

It was not a pupil who first answered the advertisement, but a theater manager who had liked Cora.

"Is that the Cora Wintle who was on tour with my Sparklers' Company?" Cora said it was. "Well, I saw your advert., and I'd like to do something for an old friend. Next summer I shall want twelve kiddies for a show I'm touring round the seaside towns. You going in for troupes?"

6

The Dancing School

Cora was not a person to let an opportunity pass. Even as the manager was speaking she could see troupes of children trained by her dancing all over the country.

"I certainly am."

"What are you calling them, dear?"

There was a tiny pause while Cora thought hard. Then the answer came to her. "Mrs. Wintle's Little Wonders."

In ten years everybody except Tom had stopped calling Cora by her Christian name. She was Mrs. Wintle or Mrs. W. wherever she went. The school was a great success, the Little Wonders were known to everybody in the theater world, and they had appeared in films and on television. When the school started Cora had been the only dancing teacher, and Pursey had done everything else in the house. But soon there were two other teachers besides Cora—Pat and Ena—and Pursey was supposed to be only the wardrobe mistress, and to employ the matrons who looked after the children when they were working. Actually Pursey never was only the wardrobe mistress, for she went on being the person everybody—staff, children and Tom—came to whenever they wanted something, were unhappy or had a worry.

Being the owner of the successful Little Wonders' Troupes changed Mrs. Wintle. There were plenty of other schools training children for the stage, and it meant pushing harder than anyone else to get her dancers known. A person who spends all his or her life pushing to get to the top gets tough as a result of working so hard. This happened to Mrs. Wintle. She became a rather frightening person. In fact, sometimes people said she had a stone where other people had a heart.

There was one person who was not at all afraid of Mrs. Wintle, and that was Dulcie. Dulcie took after her father, who was good-looking, with gray-green eyes and dark curly hair. And from being one of the prettiest babies Pursey had ever seen Dulcie grew up to be a noticeably lovely little girl, the sort of child people turn to look at in the street. Of course the moment she could toddle she had learned to dance, and so by the time she was ten and a half she danced very nicely. Unfortunately Dulcie was very conscious that she was an outstanding child, and did not try and hide it, and so was a great trial to the rest of the school. Behind her back the children called her "Little Show Off," and "That awful Dulcie-Pulsie," and the staff called her "Mrs. W.'s Little Horror." But of course they had to be as nice as they could to Dulcie's face, for none of them dared quarrel with Mrs. Wintle.

One evening early in March, when dancing lessons

had finished for the day, Mrs. Wintle came into the room Pursey used as the wardrobe, looking very unlike her usual calm hard self.

"I've got to go away, Pursey. Tom's just had a phone call. His sister-in-law has died."

Pursey laid down a pink frock on which she was working, and made sympathetic clicking noises.

"Oh dear. Very sudden, isn't it?"

"Yes, it was an accident."

Pursey tried to remember the little she had heard of the Lennox relations.

"Aren't there two little girls?"

"Yes, about Dulcie's age. Rachel and Hilary. That's why I'm going. It's so tiresome, but it looks as if we may have to bring Rachel here. We have no responsibility for Hilary; she is an adopted child. I shall arrange to have her sent to a home."

2

RACHEL AND HILARY

Rachel and Hilary lived in Folkestone in a shabby house with a tiny garden at the back. Each summer their mother had taken in boarders, and in the winter too, when anyone wanted to stay. Rachel and Hilary did not think the house shabby, for it was home and they loved it, but they did think it was nicer when they had it to themselves. Rachel had once said so.

"It's so nice, Mummie, when it's only us."

"I couldn't agree more, darling," her mother had answered, "but it means dull food, and no fun."

Rachel had been leaning against her mother's chair. When her mother said that she had laid her face against her hair.

"Silly Mummie! As if Hilary and I mind about food and fun. We only want you."

Hilary had been lying on the floor looking at a magazine a visitor had left behind. Now she said:

"I don't mind giving up my dancing lessons if that would help."

That had made Rachel and her mother laugh, for it was no sacrifice to Hilary to give up any kind of work, whether it was school lessons, dancing classes, or helping in the house. Rachel's mother said:

"That's one thing we shall never give up. Rachel and I are expecting to be kept in luxury by our star ballerina."

Hilary had started proper dancing lessons when she was eight. This came about in a rather interesting way. The teacher who taught games and physical exercise at the school the girls went to had appeared one day at the boarding house and asked to see Hilary's mother.

"I'm not really her mother," Rachel's mother had

explained. "She is not Hilary Lennox, though that's what we call her. She's adopted."

"Do you know anything about her?" the teacher asked.

Mrs. Lennox led the way into her kitchen, where she was cleaning spoons and forks.

"I don't know why you want to know, but sit down and, if you don't mind my getting on with my work, I'll tell you all about her. My husband was George Lennox."

"The film star?"

Mrs. Lennox nodded. "Yes, only he wasn't a film star for very long. When we were first married he was a poor, struggling actor."

The teacher helped in the work by piling the cleaned spoons in their proper heaps—tablespoons here, dessert spoons there, and so on. Then she said:

"Did he become famous all in a night?"

"It was after a television play. He was seen by a film man and given a screen test, and the next moment he was off to Hollywood."

"Did you go too?"

Mrs. Lennox nodded. "I sometimes think Rachel has lived on a seesaw. She was four at the time. We left our horrid little flat near the B.B.C., stepped on an airplane and found ourselves in a world of orange trees, swimming pools, endless sunshine, up to a point as many pretty clothes as we wanted, grand spoons and forks like these, large motor cars, everything. That lasted two years."

The teacher leaned over for some teaspoons Mrs. Lennox had just cleaned.

"What happened next?"

"George adopted Hilary."

"Why?" the teacher asked.

"Well, for one reason she was the same age as Rachel, and he thought it would be nice for Rachel to have someone to play with. The other reason was that she was an orphan; both her parents were killed in a hurricane."

"A hurricane!" said the teacher. "How awful. Did you know who they were?"

"Oh yes, George had known the father quite well. He was an assistant film director; the mother was a dancer."

"A dancer, was she? That explains a lot."

Mrs. Lennox looked surprised.

"Does it? In no time Hilary was as much one of the family as Rachel. Then George got an offer to make a film in England. We had got rid of the flat near the B.B.C. of course, so we decided the two children and I should go home at once and find somewhere for us to live near the film studio. We sailed the next week on the *Queen Elizabeth*. George was to fly over."

The teacher remembered the rest of that story. It had been headline news when George Lennox, the film star, was killed in an airplane crash.

"I'm so sorry," she said.

Mrs. Lennox turned a tablespoon around so that the light shone on the back of it.

"George hadn't been a star long enough to have saved any money, and the children were only seven. I had to make a home for them. I thought it would be healthy here, so with what money there was I took this house and advertised for boarders. I can't say we've got rich on it, but it does keep us."

The teacher thought Mrs. Lennox looked very tired.

"It must be hard work."

"It is, but I engage someone for housework in the summer if we are full. Rachel is a wonderful help, and at least both children are well and happy."

The teacher thought of the children. Serious, brown-eyed, straight-haired Rachel, with the high cheekbones which she had inherited from her father, and the moonlight-fair, curly-haired, pink and white Hilary.

"They certainly look splendid, and of course they're happy, though I think Rachel worries about you."

Mrs. Lennox laughed. Then she said:

"Rachel is a born worrier. She thinks it is her job to take her father's place and to look after Hilary and me."

The teacher looked again at Mrs. Lennox, and could see why Rachel worried.

"Haven't you any relations who could have helped when your husband was killed?"

"I've nobody. My husband had a brother named Tom who's an artist. I should think he's a dear, but from what George told me he has a terrifying wife. She runs some kind of a stage agency, I think. Anyway, all the money is hers, and they have a child called Dulcie to keep. Even so, Tom wrote to say I was to let him know if I couldn't manage and he would find a way to help. Luckily I haven't had to bother him. We write to each other occasionally."

The teacher came to the point of her visit.

"I'm afraid what I have come about may cost a little, but I think it will be worth it in the end. I want you to allow me to take Hilary to a dancing teacher. I think she has talent. If she has, I thought you might consider having her trained as a dancer. I feel more sure than ever, now you have told me her history, that an expert ought to see her."

Mrs. Lennox had finished cleaning the spoons and forks. She packed the cleaning materials away.

"What will it cost?" she asked the teacher.

"Not a great deal. If Madame thinks Hilary worth training I will explain you can't pay much. I'm sure she will understand."

Hilary was taken to a Madame Raine, a very good teacher of dancing. She agreed that Hilary seemed to have possibilities, and said she would take her on approval for a year. The classes would be on Saturday mornings, and in Hilary's case would only cost two-and-six a lesson.

Somehow Mrs. Lennox had found the weekly half-crowns, though it had meant going without something else. Rachel took Hilary to her classes, and listened to all that was said, and it was she who saw to it that Hilary worked.

Just after Hilary's ninth birthday Madame Raine asked to see Mrs. Lennox, so the next Saturday morning she got the shopping and the housework done early and went with the two little girls to Hilary's dancing class.

Madame Raine sent Hilary to change. She allowed Rachel to stay, so she heard what was said.

"I believe Hilary to have talent. She is not, alas, a worker, but she cares for dancing more than she will admit. I would like this year to have her for half an hour each evening. Next year I shall, with your permission, take her for an audition to The Royal Ballet

School. If they accept her I shall apply to the county for a scholarship for her, which would mean she would cost you almost nothing."

Mrs. Lennox looked worried. Somehow Hilary must have her classes. But where was the money coming from?

"What will half an hour a day cost?"

The dancing teacher looked at Mrs. Lennox's shabby, much-cleaned and mended coat, at her gloves, which had a last-year's-put-away look, at her face, which had too many lines for a woman who she guessed was only a little over thirty, and at her hair which was already turning gray.

"Nothing at all. My reward will be that someday I may see Hilary dancing at Covent Garden, and be able to say: 'I gave that girl her first lessons.' "

All that year and the beginning of the next year Hilary, with Rachel for company, went to her dancing class every afternoon after school. For half an hour she struggled with battements, frappés, and pliés at the barre, or with center practice with arm exercises. Each day the dancing mistress did not only see that Hilary understood what she was learning, but that Rachel did, too.

"You can be a great help, Rachel," Madame said. "You can make Hilary see why she has to work so hard, and to understand that I am aiming at the

17

very best for her." She smiled so that what she said did not sound unkind. "Hilary might easily admire cart-wheels and high kicks, you would never allow that, would you?"

Rachel really had begun to grasp what was meant by "posture" and "line" and could see when a series of movements looked lovely, and when they did not, so she was able to say truthfully:

"Never."

Two weeks before Hilary's audition for The Royal Ballet School Mrs. Lennox fell down the stairs, and was taken to a hospital. Because two little girls could not be alone in the house it was arranged that a Mrs. Arthur was to move in to look after them. Mrs. Arthur was very kind to Hilary, and would have been kind to Rachel, only Rachel did not want anyone to be kind to her. The doctor who had taken Mrs. Lennox to the hospital was a sensible man, and he knew it was much better for Rachel to know something terrible was going to happen than to keep worrying that it might. So she knew, the very day her mother went to the hospital, that she was never coming back. But she was the only one who did. Neither Hilary nor Mrs. Arthur was told. Because she knew before it happened Rachel was able to get used to the idea, so much so that on the day two weeks later when her mother did die she had cried most of the tears she had in her. To protect herself from people talking about her mother, and being nice, she hid herself away behind a please-leave-me-alone face which looked sulky.

Mrs. Arthur not only did not understand Rachel's expression but was quite shocked by her. It was much easier for Mrs. Arthur to understand Hilary, who on hearing the news threw herself into her arms, crying as if she would never stop.

The doctor called that afternoon and saw Rachel alone. He quite understood why she looked sulky, and pulled her onto his knee and put his arm around her.

"Your mother was conscious for a minute, and she sent you a message. You are to see that Hilary goes on with her dancing. By the way, do you know your Uncle Tom?"

Rachel felt better with the doctor's arm around her. She leaned against him.

"Daddy's brother. He's an artist. His wife is called Aunt Cora."

"That's right. Mrs. Arthur telephoned your uncle this afternoon. Your Aunt Cora is coming here tomorrow. I think you are going to live with them."

Rachel shot off the doctor's knee.

"Without Hilary?" she asked.

The doctor spoke in a quiet, don't-get-in-a-fuss voice.

"We hope Hilary is going to be taken by The Royal Ballet School. She will be a boarder then, you know."

"But where's she to be until then, and where will she be during the holidays? I won't go to Uncle Tom and Aunt Cora unless she comes too."

The doctor held out a hand, and Rachel, almost too miserable to walk, allowed herself to be drawn back into the shelter of his arm.

"You have got to be brave, Rachel, and let other people make the best possible plans for you. But I'll tell you something to cheer you up. Madame whatever her name is who teaches Hilary to dance, is going to invite her to stay with her for the time being. And here is a scheme of mine: I have a big house, and I thought perhaps next holidays both you and Hilary could stay with me."

Rachel struggled to be sensible and to see that everybody was trying to be kind. But all she could see was herself going without Hilary to live with a strange uncle and aunt. Her head fell on to the doctor's shoulder, and she cried and cried and cried.

3

MRS. WINTLE GOES TO
FOLKESTONE

Mrs. Wintle was a busy woman and she had no wish to waste a day at Folkestone, but it was certain, she thought, that Tom would muddle things, so it would be quicker in the end to go herself. She caught an early train and during the journey planned Rachel's future. She would arrange with Mrs. Arthur to stay on until a home had been found for Hilary, then she must pack Rachel's clothes and bring her to London.

Nobody knew what train Mrs. Wintle was catching, so when her taxi stopped at the gate no one was there to greet her. Hilary was in the garden supposedly hanging tea cloths on the line to dry, Rachel was making beds, and Mrs. Arthur was planning luncheon. Mrs. Arthur heard the taxi and went to the window.

"Rachel," she called up the stairs, "tidy yourself. Here's your aunt." Then she took off her apron and went to the front door.

Hilary was cheerful by nature, but that morning she had gone into the garden feeling low. Suddenly a little puff of wind smelling of spring blew up her nose, and at once all the lowness left her and she felt her spirits shoot up in the air like a firework. Instead of hanging the wet tea cloths on the line to dry she took one in each hand and danced with them around the garden, pretending that she was a butterfly and they were her wings. It was the sort of dancing she called dancing but that Madame Raine had asked Rachel to see she did not do. It was, however, just the sort of dancing Mrs. Wintle called dancing. As it happened she saw Hilary doing it, for Mrs. Arthur led her into the sitting room which looked out on to the garden.

"Good gracious me," she said. "My niece dancing!"

Mrs. Arthur went to the window. She did not know about the Wonders, so she thought Mrs. Wintle was surprised that there should be dancing at so sad a time. It never struck her that the note in the aunt's voice was pleasure. She made clicking disapproving sounds.

"That's not your niece, that's Hilary. A dear little girl, but I must say she has forgotten herself this morning." She rapped on the window.

Hilary stopped dancing, looked up and saw two faces at the window. Pretending to feel ashamed, she went to the line and began hanging up the tea cloths. Inside she was not a bit ashamed, but glad she had danced the wrong kind of dancing, for it made her feel better all over.

Mrs. Wintle had learned not to show what she was feeling, for it was a help not to look as if she cared if managers booked her Little Wonders or some other teacher's children for their shows. Now, as she talked to Mrs. Arthur about Rachel, there was no sign that she was thinking about Hilary. The child was pretty, and had talent. She would, as soon as she was old enough for a license, make a splendid Little Wonder.

But she had said she did not want her, that she was
to be sent to a home. Would it be possible to go back
on that? Then there was Dulcie to consider. She must
not have a rival. But that was hardly likely; Dulcie was
outstanding.

"I wish really," Mrs. Arthur was saying, "that
Hilary was your niece . . . such a dear little girl and
so talented. They hope she is going to The Royal
Ballet School. I'm afraid Rachel is rather a hard little
thing. You wouldn't believe it but when I told her
the sad news all she said was 'Just fancy! I'll go and
have my bath now.' "

"The Royal Ballet School," thought Mrs. Wintle.
"Not if I know it." Out loud she said: "Curious. Perhaps she didn't get on with her mother."

Mrs. Arthur was just going to say she was sure that
was not true when the door opened and Rachel came
in.

That morning the children had worn one of their
usual winter school outfits, pleated gray skirts and
jerseys. Hilary's jersey was pale blue, and Rachel's
was the color of blackberry juice. Mrs. Arthur, when
she saw what Rachel was wearing, had nodded in a
we-understand-each-other way at her and had said:
"Very nice, dear. Most suitable."

Rachel had squirmed at Mrs. Arthur's nod.

"Suitable for what?" she said in a nearly rude voice.

Mrs. Arthur was determined to be patient.

"Mourning's out of fashion, but there are times when we feel like wearing quiet colors, aren't there, dear?"

Rachel had not answered that. But, comb in hand, tidying up to meet her aunt, she had thought: "Suppose Aunt Cora thinks I'm wearing this for mourning? Suppose Aunt Cora talks about Mummie? I won't bear it. I simply won't." In a second she had crossed the room and was rummaging in a drawer where her mother had put away last summer's cotton frocks.

Rachel had grown a lot since last September, when the frocks were put away. The one she chose to wear now had been on the skimpy side even then, and it was a glorious marigold color.

Because of the marigold frock, and the extra sulky expression Rachel was wearing to keep her aunt from prying, Mrs. Wintle's first impression of Rachel was a very unfortunate one. Obviously any child who came to live under her roof had to be considered as a Little Wonder of the future, and nothing could have looked less like a Wonder than Rachel at that moment.

Being unhappy and having cried so much had taken all the color from Rachel's cheeks and given her eyes the bulgy look of somebody getting over a cold. When her mother had been there to do it for her Rachel's

25

hair was worn in plaits twisted round her head, which suited her very well. Now, because she could not manage the pinning up, the plaits stuck out at each side of her head, which was most unbecoming. Nor was that all. Being unhappy had taken away her appetite at the right times, and made her hungry at the wrong ones, so she was mostly eating bread and jam between meals. This had given her pimples—one large one on her chin, a little one on one cheek, and the beginning of another on her nose.

So what Mrs. Wintle saw was an angular little girl of ten, with a white, spotty, scowling face, plaits jutting out on each side of her head, wearing a cotton frock which was much too tight and so short that it was inches above her knees.

Mrs. Authur prided herself on never losing her head. Now, though she was horrified and puzzled by Rachel's appearance, her voice did not show it.

"This is your Aunt Cora, dear. Come and give her a nice kiss."

Mrs. Wintle was not the kissing type.

"Hullo, dear," she said in a would-be friendly voice. "You know, I suppose, that you are coming to live with me."

Rachel did not like the look of her Aunt Cora and she was afraid she might cry, so she scowled more than ever to hold back her tears.

"I knew I was coming to live with Daddy's brother, Uncle Tom."

Mrs. Wintle nodded.

"Quite right. But I don't suppose you know what an exciting house it is you are coming to. I keep a sort of school."

Rachel was surprised, for she had not heard a school mentioned.

"A school! I didn't know that."

"But not an ordinary school. Did you ever hear of Mrs. Wintle's Little Wonders?"

Rachel licked her lips nervously.

"No."

Mrs. Wintle never moved without advertisements of her Wonders. Now she opened her bag and passed Rachel a large shiny card. Printed on it was a photograph of twelve little girls. All were dressed alike in what Rachel and Hilary called little-girl frocks. They wore socks, shoes with ankle straps, and were all dancing on one leg while lifting the other almost as high as their heads. Underneath the photograph was written "Mrs. Wintle's Little Wonders." At the bottom of the card there was a photograph of three of the Wonders turning cartwheels.

Rachel stared at the card, wondering what to say that would not be rude. High kicks! Cartwheels! What would Madame Raine think? She was spared answering, for at that moment Hilary came into the room.

Hilary, with her cheeks pink from dancing in the garden, made as good an impression as Rachel had made a bad one.

"This is Hilary," said Mrs. Arthur. "Hilary, this is Rachel's Aunt Cora."

Hilary did not wait to find out if Rachel's Aunt Cora was a kissing sort of person. She ran to her and flung her arms around her neck.

"How do you do?"

Mrs. Wintle not only kissed Hilary but put an arm round her. What a delightful child, she thought, just the type to make a Wonder.

"So you've been learning to dance. I watched you from the window."

Hilary did not want to discuss her dance with the tea cloths in front of Rachel, so she spoke in a hurry.

"Yes, Madame Raine teaches me. She's taking me to The Royal Ballet School. If they say they'll teach me she is going to see if I can have a county scholarship."

Mrs. Wintle smiled, a smile that even Mrs. Arthur, who was not given to imagining things, thought a rather snap-you-up smile.

"It won't be necessary for you to go to The Royal Ballet School. I have a dancing school and I will teach you. It will be much nicer for you and Rachel to live in the same house, won't it?"

Before Hilary had taken in what had been said Rachel, her eyes alive with horror, and two red spots of color flaring on her cheekbones, had sprung forward as though to hit her aunt. Her words came out in a spit.

"Hilary's not going to live with you. I won't have it."

Mrs. Arthur, who knew how much the children loved each other, gaped at Rachel. Aunt Cora, because she trained so many Wonders, thought that she understood. She looked meaningly at Mrs. Arthur.

"I'm afraid there's a green-eyed monster here." She held Hilary more closely to her. "You'd like to be one of my Little Wonders, wouldn't you, dear? And I shall like to have you to train. I shall like having Rachel, too, when she has learned not to be jealous."

4

THE MOVE

Mrs. Wintle, having decided that she wanted Hilary as a future Wonder, had acted quickly. She had called on the solicitor who was looking after Rachel's mother's will and told him she was willing to take both children. She would take them back to London that evening.

The Move

The solicitor was most relieved.

"A dancing school! How wonderful! There is a wish expressed in the late Mrs. Lennox's will that Hilary shall be trained as a dancer. We were planning to have this carried out, but it might not have been possible, for there will be very little money even when everything is sold."

"My husband and I do not want any money," said Mrs. Wintle grandly. "The children I train start earning when they are twelve. In any case, supporting them will be our duty."

The solicitor could hardly believe his ears. He and the doctor had been worrying a lot about Rachel and Hilary, and suddenly every anxiety seemed blown away. The two children need not be separated, and Hilary would continue her dancing training. Everything just as Mrs. Lennox had wished.

"I can't tell you what a relief your news is to me."

Mrs. Wintle got up.

"That's settled then. You have our address. The children will leave with me this evening. What there is not time to pack can be sent after them."

The solicitor also got up. He took one of Mrs. Wintle's hands in both of his.

"You are very generous. I hope both children grow up to be a credit to you."

31

Mrs. Wintle thought of Rachel, and hoped very much that his wish would come true, but she doubted it.

"Thank you. My husband will of course be here for the funeral. If there is anything further you want to discuss you can talk to him."

The solicitor opened the door.

"Quite. But I'm sure there won't be. I could not imagine a happier arrangement for the two little girls."

In London Dulcie was waiting anxiously for her mother to come home. She had been annoyed that she had gone away for the day without telling her where she was going. Because she was feeling black-doggish she had tried to annoy those who taught her. Most of the Little Wonders went to the local schools, but Dulcie had a governess. She was a Mrs. Storm, who had given up teaching in schools when she married, as she needed time for shopping and household chores before she started work. This fitted in well with Dulcie's day, for her mother taught her dancing from nine to ten each morning, so lessons did not begin until half-past ten. In spite of the hours fitting so well, Mrs. Storm daily decided to give up the job.

"It's not worth it," she told her husband. "I would rather shop in my lunch hour. I've taught tiresome children before, but at least they've been surrounded by nice children. You can't think what it's like having nothing but one tiresome child to teach."

Each evening Mrs. Storm's husband persuaded her to stay on, for he was certain she would die of exhaustion if she shopped in her lunch hour. But he could see he would not be able to persuade her forever, for Dulcie was getting Mrs. Storm down.

That day had decided Mrs. Storm. Tomorrow, when Mrs. Wintle was back, she would give notice that she would not teach Dulcie any more. "And," she thought, "I'll tell her exactly what I think about her spoiled, conceited, bad-mannered child."

Pat, who in Mrs. Wintle's absence had taken Dulcie's dancing lessons, also felt like giving notice. She took her woes to the wardrobe.

Pursey looked up as Pat came in.

"Hullo, dear," she said, in her warm cozy voice. "You look tired. Come and sit down and I'll make you a nice cup of tea."

Pat sank into a chair.

"It's Dulcie. I had her for an hour alone this morning, and I've just had her again in my tap class. Do you know, Pursey, I think that child will drive me into teaching in another school."

Pursey filled the kettle.

"Nonsense, dear. Don't let yourself get upset by a little girl of ten."

"But what a little girl!" said Pat. "You don't have to teach her."

Pursey put out the teapot and two cups and saucers.

"If I did I wouldn't let her upset me. I've had plenty of naughty children to deal with in my nurseries, but I was never put out, and they soon got into my ways."

"But Dulcie isn't naughty," Pat exclaimed. "If it was naughtiness I wouldn't mind. It's what I think in the army is called 'dumb insolence.' When I was teaching her this morning I had to show her a new sequence of steps. She watched me with a sort of smile, as if to say 'Poor thing, she thinks that's dancing.' Then this afternoon at the tap class she deliberately misheard everything I said, and then when I had to stop the class and start all over again she said: 'Oh, is that what you wanted?' with all the emphasis on 'that', as if I had given the wrong instructions the first time."

Pursey put the cups and saucers on the table, and brought out her favorite comforting expression.

"Don't fret, it'll all blow over."

Of course Dulcie knew she had been tiresome all day, and mostly she was pleased about it. But as she waited for her mother to come home there was a kind of pricking worry at the back of her mind that she might have gone too far. Mrs. Storm had left after lessons looking terribly cross. It would be awkward if she would not teach her any more. Mum was hardly ever angry with her, but she might be cross about that, for she hated changing staff.

Dulcie had just reached this thought when she heard a taxi stop. She ran to the window, and watched not only her mother get out of the taxi but also two little girls. And these little girls had brought their luggage, which dancing pupils never did. With a cold feeling in her inside Dulcie watched the luggage being piled on the doorstep. Two girls could not be coming to live in the house? They simply couldn't. She was the only child who was allowed to live in the house.

A minute later Dulcie heard her mother calling. "Dulcie. Dulcie. Come down, darling."

Rachel and Hilary were so tired that they were almost asleep standing up. Since it had been decided they were going to London they had sorted out their clothes and possessions for Mrs. Arthur to pack. Up and down the stairs they had gone, carrying armfuls of books and toys. They had laid all their clothes on their beds, and tried to think which they would need, and which they would not. They had rolled things in paper, and put shoes in bags. By the time they got on the train they were glad to sit down, and even Hilary was for once silent, because she was too tired to talk.

Being so busy was a help to Rachel, for there is

nothing like having a lot to do when you are unhappy. The beginning of the packing she had done only to please Mrs. Arthur. She was sure it was a waste of time, for when the solicitor heard what Aunt Cora was planning he would not let it happen, or, if he would, the doctor would not. Then the telephone had rung, and the call had been for her. It was the doctor on the line.

"I've just heard the splendid news. I'm so glad, Rachel, that you and Hilary are not to be parted after all. And imagine your aunt teaching dancing . . . what wonderful luck!"

Rachel had tried to make him understand.

"It's the wrong kind of dancing."

But it had been hopeless. To the doctor dancing classes were dancing classes. He could not understand what she was talking about.

"Stop worrying about Hilary's dancing lessons and think of yourself. It's going to be tough for you, but keep that chin up, and as soon as you can, write to me. I shall hope to hear you are getting used to your new home."

"But . . ." Rachel interrupted.

The doctor had not heard her, for he went on:

"Here is something I want you to remember. When a dreadful thing happens to a person, as it has happened to you, there are two ways to take it. You can let it make you cross and bitter, or you can accept it, and, because you know what it's like to be hurt very badly, let it make you a nicer person. Do you understand?"

Rachel was so miserable that a lump in her throat got in the way of her answering. With great difficulty she managed a whispered "Yes."

The doctor heard her and guessed about the lump. "I wish I could see you to say good-by. But it's my hospital day, and I can't get away. Do try and remember what I have said. Don't let being unhappy spoil the nice Rachel I am fond of."

After that Rachel collected things to pack in a very whole-hearted way. There was nothing more she could do; she and Hilary were going to London. In London Hilary must learn proper dancing. She could not imagine how she would manage it, but she was sure there must be a way. In the meantime every single thing that her mother had given her must be packed. If anything was left behind somebody might think she did not want it and throw it away. People like Mrs. Arthur wouldn't know that last year's Christmas card was terribly important because it had "Love from Mummie" written on it.

Neither Rachel nor Hilary was enough awake to notice how long the drive was across London in the taxi, nor what sort of house they had arrived at. In the hall a man, who they both supposed must be Uncle Tom, kissed them and said that he was very pleased they had come to live with him. Then Aunt Cora said:

"Dulcie. Come here, darling. This is your cousin Rachel, and this is Hilary. They are going to live with us."

Rachel and Hilary looked at Dulcie in a sleepy way, and noticed how pretty she was. Then they were jolted wide awake for Dulcie, standing on the bottom step of the stairs, shouted in the rudest voice:

"I don't want any cousins to live with me. Send them away."

5

BREAKFAST

Rachel was the first to wake up the next morning.
For a second she was puzzled as to where she was.
Then, as she looked round the room, it came back to
her. This was Uncle Tom's and Aunt Cora's spare bedroom. She was just getting out of bed to see what was

outside the window when Hilary woke. She crinkled her nose, sat up, and looked round her.

"Goodness," she said, "your uncle and aunt must be awfully rich. Everything matches."

The room the girls were now in was furnished with what is called "a bedroom suite." The two beds, the wardrobe, the dressing table, the little table between the two beds, and a large round looking glass on a stand were made of mahogany. The carpet, the curtains, the eiderdowns, and the lampshades were all the same shade of green. The walls were painted a paler green.

"Just like a bedroom in a shop window," said Rachel, awed by so much grandeur.

Hilary skipped out of bed and, without putting on her dressing gown or slippers, went to the window. She pulled back the curtain and looked out.

"The street isn't grand, there are no gardens, and there are squashed-together shops."

Rachel got out of bed and joined Hilary. It was not a nice morning, for it was gray with rain about, but even when it was fine nobody could call Ford Road attractive.

Hilary's eye was caught by a bus in the distance. Its red paint made a gay splash of color through the morning grayness.

"Buses go by. I shall like that."

Breakfast

The door opened and Pursey came in carrying a tray of breakfast.

"Look at you two! No shoes on, and no dressing gowns. You'll catch your deaths. Back to bed now, and I'll turn on the heating. I turned it off last night. I don't hold with sleeping with central heating." She put the tray down on the dressing table. "I never allowed it in my nurseries. Give me a good coal fire. Put on your dressing gowns, it's nippy this morning."

Hilary, struggling into her dressing gown, looked approvingly at Pursey's back view.

"Was it you who helped us undress last night?"

Pursey laughed.

"Helped is good. Dropping, you both were. You wouldn't be in your pajamas if I hadn't put them on you. Now, into bed with you both." She came between the beds and spread table napkins over their knees. Then she went back to the dressing table and fetched two plates of cereal. "Eat that up. If I had my way it would be porridge, but Mrs. Wintle doesn't hold with porridge. She says it puts on weight."

Rachel was surprised.

"I thought that was a good thing to do."

Pursey was turning on the central heating. She straightened up and gave Rachel a quiet taking-in sort of look.

"So it is, my lamb, for anyone as skinny as you."

She came back to the beds. "You must be wondering who I am. My name is Miss Purser, but everyone calls me Pursey."

Hilary looked at Pursey's rounded shape, and her eyes laughed.

"Do you teach dancing?"

Pursey chuckled.

"That would be something to see, that would. No, I'm Mrs. Wintle's partner in the business, but I only have to do with the clothes for the theater."

The mention of dancing had made Rachel's appetite go away. She did not say anything, but instead of going on putting cereal in her mouth she messed about with it. Pursey did not seem to notice, but she did all the same, just as she had noticed Rachel's spots, and that her face was yellowish where it should have been pink. "Better change the subject," she thought, "she doesn't want to hear about the school."

"What d'you think of our spare bedroom?" Pursey asked.

"Very posh," said Hilary. "Where does Dulcie sleep?"

Pursey glanced again at Rachel; did she mind talking about Dulcie? It was clear she did not, for her eyes were interested.

"Ever so sweet a little room. Rosebuds on the walls, pink eiderdown, organdie frills. Fit for a queen."

Hilary couldn't help giggling.

"Not much like a queen last night, she wasn't."

Pursey dropped her voice to a confidential whisper.

"Very naughty she was, but you see she's an only child, and has come to think the sun rises and sets round her. But there, as I've always said, pride comes before a fall. We had a nasty fall last night, all right. It isn't like her father to say anything to her, but last night he did. She's got to apologize to you both this morning."

Hilary finished her last mouthful of cereal.

"I bet she won't."

Pursey picked up both plates.

"I'm not mentioning what isn't eaten this morning, but it's not to happen again, Rachel. We always eat what's on our plates in this house."

There were eggs to follow, and served with them was brown bread and butter.

Hilary took the top off her egg.

"Go on about Dulcie. I bet she doesn't apologize. She doesn't look the sort of child who would."

"She will." Pursey sat on Rachel's bed. "It's the quiet ones, who hardly ever create a disturbance, who always get their own way when they do." She looked at Rachel. "Your uncle's a quiet one. He wants to see you after your lessons."

"What lessons?" Rachel asked.

"Why, school lessons, of course. There's an ever so nice Mrs. Storm who teaches Dulcie, and you're to learn with her too." Out of the corner of her eyes she noticed Rachel relax. "Funny," she thought, "it must be the dancing lessons that get her. It's Hilary dancing so well, I suppose, but Rachel doesn't look the jealous sort." Out loud she said: "You go to Mrs. Storm at half-past ten. While you're at your lessons I'll get your unpacking done."

Rachel raised her eyes from her egg.

"You won't throw anything away, will you?"

"Of course not, dear, what an idea!" Pursey patted the bump in the bedclothes made by Rachel's legs. "Later I'll show you where you can find me when you want me. I'll be wanting you after meals. I've got some medicine that will put some color into those cheeks, and there'll be a nice piece of chocolate afterwards." She got up and crossed to the tray again. "Milk with a dash of tea for you both, I suppose, and there's a plate of bread and honey for when the eggs are finished. When I get back in about ten minutes I don't want to see a crumb left."

After Pursey had gone Rachel and Hilary looked at each other.

"Isn't she a gorgeous person," said Hilary.

Pursey's friendly pat on her legs had made Rachel

44

feel damp about the eyes. She looked hard at her egg, so that Hilary would not notice.

"The nicest person in London, I should think." Then she blinked the tears away and saw her egg clearly. Somehow it had all been eaten, and so had the bread and butter.

6

IN THE SCHOOLROOM

It was very seldom that anything happened which
Pursey did not know about, so she had not missed
that Mrs. Storm was in a giving-notice mood. "We
don't want any trouble of that sort this morning," she
thought. So, leaving Rachel and Hilary to finish dress-

ing, she hurried downstairs to catch Mrs. Storm before she had a chance to speak to Mrs. Wintle.

There was a room by the front door which was used as a schoolroom.

Mrs. Storm, when she saw Pursey, knew at once why she was there. She smiled at her affectionately and led the way into the schoolroom.

"Good morning, Pursey. You've guessed what I am going to do this morning. But fond of you as I am you are not going to make me change my mind."

Pursey looked as she often had when she was a children's nannie and had to argue with somebody over what she thought was right in her nursery.

"There's two more children going to learn with you."

Mrs. Storm was taking off her hat and looking at her hair in a looking glass. She swung round.

"Two more Little Wonders! If you think that's going to change my mind you're wrong."

Pursey's cozy voice could be stern sometimes.

"There's nothing the matter with most of the Wonders. They're nice hard-working children." She paused to leave time for that to sink in. "But these two aren't Wonders . . . at least, not yet they're not."

Mrs. Storm opened a drawer and got out Dulcie's school books.

"Who are they then?"

Pursey sat down and told Mrs. Storm all she knew about Rachel and Hilary.

"Mrs. Wintle says the woman who looked after them says Rachel is hard, never cried when her mother died, that it was Hilary who was upset. But Rachel doesn't look that sort to me. Mrs. W. says Hilary is a good dancer, and that Rachel is jealous of her. I can't say about that either. It may be true, or it may not. But one thing I do know, Mrs. Storm, both little girls will need friends. I'm speaking plain, but you know how it is in this house. It's Dulcie first, and always will be."

Mrs. Storm put the pile of lesson books on the table.

"Poor children, I'd like to help." Then she thought about Dulcie. "But if I stay I'll let Mrs. Wintle know I had meant to leave, and I'll tell her what I think of the way she is bringing up her child."

Pursey moved to the door, then she paused.

"It's your business, of course, Mrs. Storm, but if you can make yourself do it I'd not say anything to upset Mrs. W. this morning. The little girls will be feeling strange, and we don't want ructions their first day."

Before Mrs. Storm had time to think over what Pursey had said, and decide what to do, Mrs. Wintle was in the schoolroom.

"Good morning. You've seen Pursey, I hear, so you know about Rachel and Hilary." She sat down. "Dulcie's changing out of her dancing things, and Pursey won't bring the other two to you for five minutes."

There was a pause. Mrs. Storm could feel that Mrs. Wintle was feeling for the words she wanted to say. To fill the gap Mrs. Storm said:

"Yes, Mrs. Wintle?"

Mrs. Wintle rapped with her fingers impatiently on the table,

"It was all very sudden. But it seemed to me best to bring the children back with me last night. I telephoned of course to say they were coming, but no one had told Dulcie. They thought I would rather do it. It was a shock to the poor child when I arrived with two strange children. She said things she didn't mean. Her father was cross about it and says Dulcie is to apologize. Such nonsense, still he insists. Will you see to it, Mrs. Storm? I don't want to have anything to do with it."

Mrs. Storm was startled. Dulcie's father insisting on something. It had never happened before. She managed to keep surprise out of her voice.

"Of course."

"It only wants the word 'sorry.' I'm sure you can handle it without upsetting Dulcie. Now for plans.

The child Hilary appears to have considerable dancing talent, so I may teach her with Dulcie, or I may hand her over to Pat or Ena."

"Has she now," thought Mrs. Storm. "I wonder how Dulcie will like that." Out loud she said:

"I see."

"The other child, Rachel, is unattractive. I must see what can be done with her. She may be good enough for one of my less talented troupes, or I may use her as an understudy."

Mrs. Wintle paused, so Mrs. Storm said again:

"I see."

"Rachel will attend the usual beginners' classes in the evenings, and on Saturdays. For the moment at any rate she is not worth wasting time on, so when Dulcie and Hilary are at dancing classes perhaps you would arrange homework for Rachel. She can work in here until you arrive."

There was another pause, during which Mrs. Storm thought of the unattractive Rachel. Poor child, how depressing if you were plain by nature, to have to grow up to be either a Little Wonder or an understudy to one. It was at that moment Mrs. Storm decided to bear with Dulcie and stay on.

"I see."

Mrs. Wintle had noticed the pause and misunderstood it.

"These are only temporary plans. If you find Rachel tiresome, there is no reason why you should teach her. As she will not be having special classes she can go to the local school." She looked at her watch and got up. "The children will be here in a moment. Don't make too much of the apology. Poor little Dulcie, she will hate it so."

Rachel and Hilary, with Pursey, arrived in the schoolroom only a second before Dulcie shot in. Dulcie was wearing a scarlet frock and scarlet shoes, and her cheeks were scarlet. Although she was cross she still looked prettier than any child Rachel and Hilary had met before. They stared at her admiringly. Dulcie stood in front of them, her chin in the air.

"My father says I am to say I was sorry I was rude to you last night. I don't think I was rude, I think I was just truthful, for I said what I meant. But if you think I was rude I'm sorry."

Mrs. Storm was about to tell Dulcie that it was a very poor apology, but Pursey gave her a look over the children's heads as if to say, "Let that pass." Aloud she said:

"This is Rachel, Mrs. Storm, and this is Hilary. And now I'll leave you, for you'll want to be getting on with the lessons."

Mrs. Storm had placed four chairs around the table.

"You sit here, Rachel, and you here, Hilary. We'll

have to have a sort of examination this morning to see what you know. How old are you both?"

"Ten," said Hilary. "Rachel was ten in January, and I was ten five days ago."

"January and March," said Mrs. Storm. "Dulcie will be eleven in November, so you are the eldest, Dulcie. We'll start with arithmetic. Where have you got to, Rachel?"

Because Dulcie had been Mrs. Storm's only pupil, and Rachel had learned in a class with more than thirty other children, Dulcie was ahead of her at lessons. This put Dulcie in a good temper and made her forget about having had to apologize.

"If I've got to have you here," she said to Rachel, "I'm glad you're only just behind me at lessons. It'll be fun beating you."

It was half-past eleven, the time when there was a break for milk and biscuits. Mrs. Storm passed the biscuits around.

"I expect Rachel will soon catch you up, Dulcie. She's not far behind you, and she's going to do some extra work for me while you and Hilary are at your morning dancing class."

This was the first Dulcie had heard of Hilary being able to dance.

"You won't be dancing with me, Hilary. I'm much too advanced for you."

"How d'you know?" Hilary asked.

Dulcie found that difficult to answer. It was one of those things nobody in the school argued about. She was the best dancer and that was that. Now she said:

"I've been learning all my life."

Hilary did not care really if she danced as well as Dulcie or not, but no child was going to talk to her in a proud voice.

"I've been learning quite a long time. And, as a matter of fact, if I hadn't come here I was going to The Royal Ballet School."

Dulcie caught her breath. The Royal Ballet School! It could not be true.

"I bet they wouldn't have had you."

Hilary shrugged her shoulders.

"You may be right, but Madame Raine, who taught me, thought they would."

"Can you do tap and acrobatics?"

"No, but I'll soon learn."

Rachel could bear the argument no longer. She got out of her chair and ran to Hilary. She took hold of her shoulders and shook her until Hilary was pink in the face.

"Shut up! Shut up! Shut up! You aren't to learn acrobatics or tap, and you aren't going to be a Little Wonder."

Dulcie lay across the table, her chin on her folded

arms, her eyes glued on Rachel and Hilary. This would be something to tell Mum. Who would have to apologize now? Aloud she said:

"Why isn't Hilary to be a Wonder?"

Rachel let go of Hilary and, with her eyes looking as if coals were burning in them, she faced Dulcie.

"Because I say so. It's me who decides now what Hilary will do."

7

RACHEL IN TROUBLE

It was, Rachel discovered, all very well to talk in a big
grand way, but when you were ten years old, and had
been taken in by an uncle and aunt as a kindness,
nobody paid the slightest attention to what you
wished.

After Rachel had said Hilary was not to learn to be

a Wonder, Mrs. Storm had started lessons again as if nothing was wrong. But it was rather like spreading a clean cloth over a table to hide a mess underneath. It did not make the mess any less real. Rachel, after being excited by being angry, felt sick and looked it. Hilary, trying to pretend she was not, kept looking at Dulcie, wishing she could finish arguing with her about who danced best. Dulcie was thinking how she would tell her mother every word Rachel had said. Mrs. Storm was talking about *Twelfth Night* as if she thought all three children were listening, when she knew none of them were.

After lessons Rachel was sent to the room her Uncle Tom used as a studio. He was painting at an easel, but he stopped as soon as Rachel came in. He gave her rather a paint-smelling hug.

"Hullo, my dear. I hope you and Hilary are settling in. I'm sorry about last night. Dulcie didn't mean to be unkind. I hope she's told you she's sorry."

Rachel did not quite know how to answer either about the settling in or Dulcie, so she went over to the easel and looked at the picture Uncle Tom was painting. It was for once a money-earning picture, a portrait of a fat man. It was not an easy picture to say anything nice about, because the fat man was ugly and seemed to Rachel an odd person to want to paint. Then she had an idea.

"Is he a relation?" she asked.

Uncle Tom laughed.

"No, thank goodness. He's what's known as a city magnate. This portrait's going to hang in what's called a board room. When it's finished I shall be able to paint more pictures that I like painting, like this one." Uncle Tom pulled out a canvas from a pile against a wall and turned it to face Rachel. She looked at it for some time before understanding what it was a picture of, then she saw that it was a public park with people lying on the grass.

Uncle Tom laid a hand on Rachel's shoulder.

"Look, old lady, I am very keen that you should be happy with us. If there's anything you want, or would like to talk over, you'll usually find me here at some time each day. I'll help any way I can."

Rachel looked up at Uncle Tom. Sudden hope made her eyes shine.

"Can I ask you something now?"

"Of course."

"Would you tell Aunt Cora that she's not to teach Hilary to dance? Say that she's to send her to The Royal Ballet School."

Even before she had finished speaking Rachel saw it was no good. Uncle Tom's face had a hopeless look.

"Oh dear, if only you had asked me something else.

I can't interfere with the dancing side of things. Your aunt wouldn't listen to me."

Rachel stared at the floor, swallowing hard. Why had Uncle Tom said he would help if the moment he was asked to do something he said he couldn't? Somehow she swallowed the lump in her throat, but her voice came out rather small from having fought to get rid of it.

"I see. Thank you very much for showing me your pictures. I expect I ought to go and get washed for lunch."

Luncheon was eaten in the school canteen, which was in the basement. There was a counter at one end, where the staff and Wonders could buy a hot meal.

Rachel and Hilary took a tray to the counter and were handed their food already on plates. It was cottage pie, with a milk pudding and prunes to follow.

Hilary nudged Rachel.

"Where do you think we ought to sit? Ought we to sit with them?"

"Them" were Dulcie and her mother. They were sitting at the end of one of the tables, with their heads close together, deep in conversation.

"They don't look as if they were expecting us," Rachel whispered.

"Thank goodness," said Hilary. She led the way to

the table at which Mrs. Storm and Pursey, also deep in conversation, were sitting. "Can we sit here?"

Pursey broke off what she was saying and beamed at them both.

"Of course, my lambs. I ought to have been looking out for you, but we're so used to this canteen we forget others aren't. Now you eat that cottage pie while it's hot, Rachel dear."

After luncheon Rachel went to the wardrobe to have her medicine. While Pursey was pouring it out she decided that she was the person who would understand about Hilary's dancing.

"I was wondering, Pursey, do you think you could make Aunt Cora see that Hilary shouldn't be here?"

Pursey had heard from Mrs. Storm all about the row in the schoolroom, and had been wondering if she should say anything. Rachel's having brought up the subject of Hilary decided her. She spoke severely.

"Look, dear. I don't know what's in your mind about Hilary, but of course I've heard what was spoken this morning, for nothing is a secret in this place. You said it was for you to decide what dancing Hilary learned, didn't you?"

Rachel was still hoping to make Pursey understand. "Yes, and I was quite right. You see . . ."

Pursey, though she was sorry for Rachel, thought

she was behaving badly. She held up a hand to stop her from saying more.

"You were not right. It's very good of your aunt and uncle to take Hilary, for she's nothing to them, and it's a wonderful chance for her, seeing that she's studied dancing."

Rachel could have stamped her foot at such stupidity.

"It's not a wonderful chance, it's a bad chance. I don't want Hilary to do any dancing here. Actually, I don't want her to be here at all."

Pursey's voice was really stern.

"Now listen, dear. You're speaking wrongly, and you know it. I daresay it does seem hard that Hilary's quite the dancer, while you've got it all to learn, but she's your adopted sister, and that's not a nice way to feel about a sister."

Rachel gasped.

"But . . ."

Pursey held up her hand.

"No, dear, let me finish, and then we won't talk of this again. You've had a sad time, and I quite understand how you feel. These are your relatives and not Hilary's. But that isn't nice, is it? You wouldn't want to think poor little Hilary had nowhere to go."

Rachel could not believe that nice Pursey could mean what she was saying. She could not really think she did not want Hilary to live with her. Everybody knew she wanted Hilary. Aunt Cora knew it was because of The Royal Ballet School. She must have told Pursey. How could she make Pursey understand?

"I would rather live without Hilary if it meant she could . . ."

But Pursey refused to listen.

"None of that talk, dear. Live without Hilary indeed!" She had found her yard measure. "Now, let's measure you. You want practice dresses, one off and one on, and then there's shoes to get, those for tap, and those for stage . . ."

Rachel stared at the yard measure.

"I'm not going to learn to dance."

Pursey went on measuring.

"Of course you are, dear. How else will we make a Little Wonder of you?"

8

SETTLING IN

Mrs. Wintle was famous for her troupes of dancers. Sometimes she got an engagement for a child as a principal, but it was unusual. When her telephone bell rang it was usually a manager saying "I want ten little blondes," or "I'm looking for six really smart kiddies, Mrs. W." So the aim of the school was to teach all the pupils to dance alike. Of course all the children were not equally good, so they were graded into three standards. It was from number one group that children were sent to auditions when a manager asked for really smart kiddies. The number two group danced in troupes of usually twelve. Number three group was used on tour in not very big towns, or in large troupes where not too high a standard was expected, or as understudies. Nobody liked belonging to number three group, everyone tried to climb out of it as quickly as possible.

There were four classes all the pupils had to attend. Tap dancing, musical comedy, acrobatics and singing. As well, there were ballet classes for a few promising children. The Little Wonders came to their classes immediately after ordinary school finished. They began attending classes when they were about six years of age, so they were usually working in a group by the time they were eight.

Poor Rachel, who had done no dancing, had to work with the beginners. As she was two years older than the eldest of them, she felt as tall as a giant, and as sprawly about the legs as a Daddy-Long-Legs.

For dancing, all the Wonders wore bright green practice tunics, white socks, and patent-leather shoes with straps around the ankle. These shoes were known throughout the school as "awkward Adas." For tap they had another pair of awkward Adas, with steel tips to the toes.

It had been decided that Hilary must keep up her ballet dancing.

"You never know," Mrs. Wintle said to Pat and Ena, "it might get her a little solo. You'd better take her, Pat, for an hour each morning while I'm teaching Dulcie."

Pat had diplomas for teaching ballet, she taught Dulcie, and she had a class for ballet on Saturday mornings. But ballet was very much a side line in the school. As a form of dancing it was not so generally useful as musical comedy or tap. So it was good news for Pat that she was to teach Hilary. It would be nice to have a pupil who had been carefully taught before she came to her.

"We ought to start acting classes, Mrs. W., if we have many more children like . . ." Pat was going to say "Hilary," but she remembered just in time whom she was talking to, so she said, "Dulcie and Hilary."

Ena supported her.

"We ought, Mrs. W. Dulcie would make a lovely principal in a children's play, or in a pantomime. It's too early to say yet, of course, but we might do something with Hilary too."

Mrs. Wintle did not altogether like that. It was all

very well to say Dulcie might be a star, but there was no need to bracket Hilary with her.

"I think Dulcie's a natural little actress, but I'll tell Mrs. Storm to give her extra elocution. Perhaps next year the child might take outside elocution classes."

As well as her morning ballet Hilary had either an hour's tap or an hour's acrobatics and musical comedy each evening. On Saturdays she had the general singing class and two hours' dancing. Because she had been well grounded in ballet she was too good for the beginners' classes, so she was put straight away into group two, and very hard work she found it. But some of her lessons made her laugh.

"Just like horses we look," she told the other girls after a musical comedy class, "so prancy and knees-up looking."

Acrobatics were fun to her too. Every spare minute she was trying to turn a cartwheel.

"Watch this child you taught, Madame Raine," she would think as she shot forward on one hand. "What would you say if you saw her now?"

Hilary easily got used to anything, and she would have enjoyed herself in the school if it had not been for Rachel. Of course Hilary knew the sort of dancing Madame Raine had wanted her to learn. She knew, too, that Rachel's mother had agreed she was to learn that sort of dancing. But she was not a bit sure that if Rachel's mother could see her now she would not be quite pleased. After all, she had said she was having her taught to dance because someday she expected to be kept in luxury by her star ballerina. Of course the dancing she was doing now, except for Pat's class, was not The Royal Ballet School sort of dancing, but what did that matter? She was being trained to be a dancer, so she could not see what Rachel was fussing about.

Ever since she had been adopted Hilary had felt as if she really was Rachel's sister. They had always shared everything, especially things to talk about, and it seemed so odd suddenly not to be able to talk about something they were both doing every day. But there was no way of making Rachel talk about dancing lessons, except her ballet class with Pat. As soon as she started to say: "Imagine, at tap this evening . . ." or something like that, Rachel turned her back on her.

"I don't want to hear. I'm not interested in your tap."

Because dancing was the obvious thing to talk about, and Rachel would not talk about it, Hilary spent less time with her. Of course the grownups noticed, and of course most of them misunderstood, and blamed Rachel.

It was not only Hilary, and not being able to do

what her mother had asked her to do, that worried Rachel. It was her own dancing classes. How they bored her, and how difficult she found them. It was not that she did not try, she did, but her feet simply would not obey her. She tried so hard sometimes that she woke herself up in the night kicking up her legs, as Ena was trying to teach her to do in musical comedy classes. But worst of all was tap. Even the smallest beginner seemed to understand tap, and some of them were quite clever at it, but not Rachel. "Brush," she would mutter, "brush," trying desperately to get the feel of the steel on her shoe. But when she tried to brush one foot in front of the other her shoe either did not touch the ground, or instead of brushing, it scratched the floor. Nobody could like not being able to do something that babies of six could manage. In fact Rachel was beginning to feel a most inferior person.

To make Rachel feel more inferior, in spite of Pursey's medicine, she still looked pale and still had spots, neither of which look well against a bright green tunic. Then, though Hilary had tried several times to pin up Rachel's plaits in the way Rachel's mother had done, she had not succeeded. So Rachel's plaits still stuck out on each side of her head. In a school given up to trying to turn children into Little Wonders it was not surprising that people sighed when they looked at Rachel. Nor was it surprising that Rachel knew they were sighing, and why.

The best part of the day for Rachel was lessons. Mrs. Storm, because it was not her business to turn Rachel into a Wonder, thought about her as an ordinary little girl. She felt sorry for her, for she knew it was no fun being the plainest child. She had been a plain child herself. Luckily, as she now knew but of course Rachel did not, what you looked like at school had very little to do with what you looked like when you grew up. The ugliest child often turned out a beauty. But because she knew how it felt not to be pretty she would sometimes think about Rachel. "If she was mine," she would wonder, "what would I do to improve her appearance?"

Because she was sorry for Rachel, instead of leaving her alone to do homework for an hour Mrs. Storm would, when she could cut a few minutes off her shopping, get to the schoolroom early. She could then talk to Rachel before Dulcie and Hilary had finished changing after their dancing lessons.

People cannot talk to each other every day without getting to know a little about each other. Unfortunately, although Rachel tried to explain, Mrs. Storm did not know a thing about real ballet. But she could understand very well somebody not wanting to learn to be a dancer, so she was gloriously sympathetic about musical comedy, acrobatics and what Rachel called "That awful tap."

"It's horrid for you, but I expect you'll soon pick it up, and then things won't be so bad. What we must try and find is something you do like doing, to make up for the dancing classes. Was there anything you were especially fond of at Folkestone?"

Rachel tried to think.

"I liked helping in the house."

"That's most unusual and ought to be useful anywhere, but oddly enough I don't think it's of much use in this house."

Rachel sighed.

"It isn't. Do you know, Pursey even makes our beds. Hilary and I have been making our own for years."

"Wasn't there anything you liked at school?"

Rachel made herself think back to Folkestone, a place she had been trying not to think about.

"Once we acted a piece of *Toad of Toad Hall*. I was Ratty. I liked that awfully. Hilary was a Wild Wood-er."

Mrs. Storm was delighted.

"How lucky you like acting. Mrs. Wintle wants Dulcie to have extra elocution, so we'll have an acting class."

Rachel looked doubtful.

"Aunt Cora wouldn't want to come and watch, would she?"

Mrs. Storm laughed.

"Goose, why do you care if she does? Anyway, you might be good, and if you were I should be proud to have her watch you."

Rachel was remembering how much her mother had enjoyed watching her be Ratty. Aunt Cora would not enjoy watching her act anything. In fact, if she was as good as Dulcie Aunt Cora might be angry.

9

GOOD FRIDAY

Rachel had one hope about Hilary's dancing. One day Madame Raine would come to London and she would say to Aunt Cora: "I've come to take Hilary to The Royal Ballet School." When she thought this Rachel imagined Aunt Cora answering in a humble voice: "Of course, Madame Raine. Hilary shall go with you at once."

Although the term went by and Madame Raine did not appear, Rachel never lost hope. One day she would come. She must, she absolutely must. Then Rachel kept her promise to the doctor, and wrote him a letter. She could not say she was happy with Aunt Cora, but she did say she liked her school lessons, and that she was fond of Pursey. Then she told him what a lot of dancing she had to do, and that Hilary was doing an extra ballet class, as well as the ordinary school dancing. It was the doctor's answer that made Rachel give up forever her hope of Madame Raine coming to the rescue.

"My dear Rachel,

"I was so pleased to get your nice letter. I am glad you like Mrs. Storm and Miss Purser. I am sorry you hate dancing, but I expect the exercise is good for you, even if you don't learn very much.

"Yesterday Madame Raine who used to teach Hilary came to see me. She wanted news of Hilary, so I showed her your letter. She is, I think, disappointed to lose Hilary as a pupil, but of course she is glad that you two are together.

"Much love, my dear. Keep that chin up.

"Your affectionate friend,

"THE DOCTOR"

The doctor, not understanding about dancing, had believed truly that Madame Raine had come to see him only to get news of the children. But what she had really come for was to find out what sort of dancing Hilary was doing at Rachel's aunt's school. And what the doctor said had made her see that she could not possibly interfere. He was certain that the best thing was for Hilary and Rachel to be brought up together. So rather sadly she had gone away, deciding that her dreams for Hilary would have to be forgotten.

Of course Rachel could not know what Madame Raine was thinking and so she had to believe that she, like everyone else, had stopped trying. As she accepted this, Rachel knew there was only one thing left to do. Hilary must be made ambitious. She was learning proper ballet with Pat. If she worked hard at that and not too hard at musical comedy, tap, and acrobatics there was still hope.

Quite soon it was Easter. But holidays did not mean that one had a long holiday at Mrs. Wintle's school. Ordinary lessons stopped, but because the Wonders were not attending school they had more dancing classes. There was a long week-end holiday from Thursday night until Tuesday morning, but that was all. Rachel had not liked to think about Easter because at Folkestone her mother had always made

Easter Day fun. But she need not have worried. Pursey knew all about proper things for proper days.

"What did you and Hilary do of a Good Friday?" she asked Rachel one lunch time when she was pouring out her medicine.

Rachel chose her piece of chocolate.

"First there was the children's service. Then we packed sandwiches, hot cross buns and a banana and joined some other children, and went by bus to a wood to pick primroses to decorate the church."

"Very right and proper," said Pursey. "And if it's fine we'll do the same. Of course it's quite a way out of London to get primroses, but we'll manage."

Churchgoing had been rather vague since Rachel and Hilary had come to London. They had gone several times to morning service with Pursey, which they had found much duller than a children's service. On Palm Sunday they had gone to a quite different church with Aunt Cora and Dulcie, and had been given palm crosses. And once when Pursey had a cold, and Aunt Cora had taken Dulcie to spend the day with relations, they had gone to church with Wanda and Yolanta, the Polish refugees who did the cooking and serving. Theirs was a quite different sort of church, with the service in a foreign language.

"Oh well," Pursey had said, "it won't hurt for once.

What I say is church is church. It's going somewhere that matters."

Good Friday was a lovely day, from start to finish. Hilary, Rachel and Pursey, carrying baskets full of lunch, and wool to tie up primroses, caught a very early train into Sussex. There they first went to the village church where a service was going on, and then into a primrose wood where they ate lunch and then got down to picking.

It was a truly superb wood. The primroses made a yellow carpet, with a pattern of dog violets and wood anemones running through them. And so many birds were singing they might have been rehearsing for a bird concert.

Picking primroses is hard work, and Pursey soon found that it "got her back," so she spread her mackintosh under a tree and sat down for a rest. Hilary became bored with picking and practiced cartwheels. Rachel alone went on pick, pick, pick until her basket was full of bunches, and the more she picked the better she felt inside herself.

When her basket was full Rachel brought it to Pursey's tree.

"Shall I put some of these in your basket?"

Pursey looked admiring.

"My, my, what a lot. Yes, do but take a rest first.

I'll pour you out some lemonade, and maybe after all that work you could find room for another hot cross bun."

Pursey made a place for Rachel on her mackintosh, and to Rachel's surprise there was room inside her for a hot cross bun.

Pursey smiled at her approvingly.

"That's what I like to see. No pecking for once."

"I don't mean to peck," Rachel apologized, "it's just that I've not been very hungry lately."

Pursey nodded.

"I know, dear. But time's a great healer."

Pursey's cozy voice fitted in with the wood and the birds, and made Rachel feel able to talk.

"Time isn't making me able to dance. Do you think I must be a Little Wonder, Pursey?"

Pursey chose her words carefully.

"Now I don't want you to misunderstand what I say, dear. When everything's sold there won't be all that money for you. So what your aunt and uncle plan is that what there is will be kept until you are grown up. That means it will be more than it is now. I don't quite understand how, but it's something called interest."

It was the first Rachel had heard about her having any money.

"Does it have to wait until I'm grown up?"

"Yes, if your uncle and aunt say it does. They're your guardians, so to speak."

"And they can do what they like?"

"What they think right is more like it."

"And what they think right is that I shall be a Little Wonder?"

Pursey paused for a long while before she answered.

"It's natural that your Aunt Cora should plan to have you trained. All the children she knows she's training. Maybe you aren't cut out for a dancer, but I'm sure she'll make something of you."

Rachel picked some dog violets growing beside the edge of Pursey's mackintosh.

"But suppose I don't want to be made something of?"

Pursey patted Rachel's shoulder.

"But you do if you think right. You've got a nice home, and no expense spared. And mind you, if by the time you're fifteen or so you still aren't taking to the Wonders, then I'm sure your aunt will see reason and let you have part of your money to train for something different."

Rachel swung round to Pursey.

"Honestly? She would let me do something different?"

Pursey hoped she had not said too much.

"Yes, but you've got to give the dancing a chance first."

Rachel was watching Hilary trying to turn a good cartwheel. Fifteen would not be too late. Hilary was still learning proper dancing each morning. She would have to talk her out of practicing acrobatics, tap and musical comedy, but it might happen. It wouldn't be so long before she was fifteen, and then she could train for something sensible, and Hilary could come and live with her, and learn to be a proper ballerina.

Rachel knelt and flung her arms around Pursey's neck.

"Angel Pursey, you can't think how much better I feel. I will try and be a Little Wonder, honestly I will. It won't seem so bad if it's only till I'm fifteen."

Pursey returned Rachel's hug, but she was worried.

"Now what have I done," she thought. "Put the cat among the pigeons, shouldn't wonder. Still, it's nice to see her smiling, bless her."

All of Easter was nice. On Easter Day there were breakfast eggs beautifully dyed by Wanda. After breakfast there was an egg hunt all over the house. The eggs had been hidden by Uncle Tom, who was such a good hider that even Dulcie got excited and forgot to be a Little Wonder, and instead rushed about like an ordinary child.

Aunt Cora's parents lived just outside London, so

after the egg hunting she and Uncle Tom and Dulcie went to spend the day with them. Hilary, watching them go, turned a cartwheel and said:

"That suits us. All the house for you and me, Rachel, Pursey, Wanda and Yolanta."

It rained in the afternoon, so after a superb Easter luncheon Wanda, Yolanta, Rachel and Hilary played hide and seek all over the house. Pursey said she was too old for hide and seek, and that she would have a nice read in her room. Actually she slept until teatime, in spite of the hide-and-seek noise, for each time the others passed her door they heard her snoring.

On Monday Uncle Tom said he was going to Hampstead Heath, and he asked the children to come with him. Aunt Cora did not want them to go, because she said Hampstead on an Easter Monday was too rough, but Pursey said:

"Lovely air at Hampstead, freshen the children up for their dancing tomorrow."

So Aunt Cora agreed that Rachel and Hilary might go, but not Dulcie.

"I'm sorry, but those two feet are too valuable to be trodden on, Dulcie darling."

Hampstead was gorgeous, with its roundabouts and swings. And Uncle Tom was the perfect companion at a fair. He believed in doing everything and, if you liked anything very much, in doing it over and over again until you were bored with it. He also believed in eating anything you fancied. So what with the things that went round, and up and down, and those which whipped around corners, and the mixture of eating, the children felt most peculiar before they were home, and were both sick in the night. Still, it had been a lovely day, and when they woke the next morning and saw the things they had won at the stalls they both agreed that being sick was worth it. Pursey, who came in to see how they were, agreed with them.

"What's being sick? Better out than in, I say. And a nice day is something to remember."

10

POCKET MONEY

With something to work for Rachel struggled hard at her dancing classes, and as a result began at last to improve. She gave up falling over her feet, and lifting her right leg when she was told to lift her left. She even began in a dim way to understand tap. She could not learn to smile while she danced, for she had to think so hard she always wore an anxious frown. But during the Easter school holidays, for the first time Pat and Ena were able to say that she was getting on.

"Rachel's improving, Mrs. W. We might be able to shift her into group three in the autumn," said Pat.

Ena agreed.

"She's working hard, and seems to put some heart into her dancing. A great change since she first came to us."

Mrs. Wintle looked upon Rachel as a duty, and could not imagine her being a pleasure.

"I'm glad she's working. It's the least she can do, seeing what we've done for her."

"I wish she'd smile more," said Pat. "She'd look so much prettier."

Mrs. Wintle made an impatient noise.

"It will take more than a smile to improve that child. She's hard and jealous by nature and it comes out in her face. Look at the way she tried to prevent me taking in Hilary, and wasn't even upset when her mother died."

It was in the Easter holidays that Rachel talked to Hilary about concentrating on her ballet classes. In term time, wet or fine, Dulcie, Rachel and Hilary had an afternoon walk with Mrs. Storm. In the holidays they still had to go out every day, but it was not always a set walk. Sometimes they went shopping with Pursey or Wanda. But one day there was no shopping and Dulcie was at the dentist, so Rachel and Hilary were sent out alone to play in the nearest park. It was very easy to say a thing in such a way that it made Hilary laugh, so Rachel started carefully.

"Do you get on much faster at ballet, with the extra classes you're having now it's holidays?"

Hilary had been about to try new acrobatics she was learning called flip-flaps. She paused, both arms up, hoping to throw herself backward to land on her hands, from which position somebody who could do flip-flaps would spring upright again.

"I suppose so. I'm having blocked ballet shoes next week."

Rachel thought it very odd of Hilary not to have told her such important news before.

"Proper ones? Like the big girls wore at Madame Raine's?"

Hilary tried her flip-flap and fell over. She spoke sitting on the grass.

"Of course. Blocked shoes are blocked shoes."

"That means you're going to dance proper dancing on your toes."

"On my pointes," Hilary corrected her. She got up and stretched up her arms again. "But it's not any

83

different. The same old exercises, frappés, battements, and all those, only on my pointes instead of demi-pointes."

Rachel waited until Hilary had tried another flip-flap. This was a better one, but it still landed her on the grass. Then she said:

"But being on your pointes at all is pretty grand. None of the Wonders, even those old enough to be working, dance on their pointes."

Hilary shrugged her shoulders.

"I don't feel grand, I just feel bored. I think in this school it's a waste of time learning ballet. None of the troupes do it."

Rachel wanted to say "But you're not going to be a Wonder forever. When I'm fifteen . . ." But she bit it back and said, instead:

"Pursey told me that Dulcie was not going to be a Wonder . . . I mean not in a troupe. She thought she would get important parts like Alice in *Alice in Wonderland,* and that's why we're doing acting with Mrs. Storm. She said Pat and Ena thought you might get proper parts too."

Hilary turned a nice cartwheel, then she skipped along beside Rachel.

"I'm not sure I'd like that. The girls say it's terrific fun being in a troupe."

It was no news to Rachel that Hilary was not ambitious, but it was the first time she had heard her actually want to join a troupe.

"Pursey says you'd earn a lot of money if you were a star child."

Hilary sighed.

"I wish I could earn now. Do you know, Rachel, we're the only children in the school who have no pocket money at all."

"We get sixpence on Sundays."

"What good's that? We have to put it in the collection plate. I asked Pursey if I could have mine in six pennies, because I thought then church could have three and me three. But Pursey said: 'I'm too old a dog for that trick,' and gave me a sixpence as usual."

Rachel was often shocked by Hilary.

"You wouldn't have stolen from the church, Hilary!"

"I don't think it would be stealing. Church money is charity, and I don't know a more important charity than us, with no pocket money at all."

"What would you buy if you had pocket money? We're given everything, even sweets," Rachel pointed out.

Rachel, struggling with her dancing classes, and her plans for Hilary, had not taken much interest in the school. The children in the beginners' class were too young for her, and she had not made friends in the groups. But Hilary, working with the Wonders in group two, had any number of friends, all of whom were swept by new fashions which cost money. Now she looked at Rachel in a despairing way. What would she buy if she had pocket money? What a question!

"Haven't you noticed that coffee whirls, which aren't sold in the canteen, are being eaten this holiday? Or that the best Wonders have a toy animal to bring to school?"

"No."

"Well, do you know a girl in group one with red hair?" Rachel shook her head. "You wouldn't. Well, she started it. She came to school one day bringing the most gorgeous little black poodle made of felt, but with all those special bits, like the end of his tail and his trousers, and the top of his head, real fur."

Rachel was impressed by that.

"She must be awfully rich to buy a toy dog with real fur."

"She is, the richest girl in the school. Her father's a hairdresser."

Hilary's ability to find things out always surprised Rachel.

"How d'you know he's a hairdresser?"

"I don't know, I just do. Anyway, her poodle started it, and since then everybody has an animal. Dogs, cats, monkeys, donkeys, all sorts, mostly little and made of felt, though some are velvet or sham fur. If I had pocket money I'd have a little rabbit, and coffee whirls too."

Hilary moved away to try another flip-flap. Watching her Rachel had an idea. Suppose she could get some pocket money and used it as a bribe, would that make Hilary work at ballet? Even as she thought about pocket money she knew who would help her to get it. Uncle Tom had said, "Oh dear, if only you had asked me something else." Well, here was "something else."

"Hilary," she called, "stop doing that. I've thought of something."

Hilary's last effort had been the nearest to a flip-flap she had managed so far, and she did not want to stop, so she turned a rather unwilling face to Rachel.

"What is it?"

"I can get you some pocket money."

In one bound Hilary was at Rachel's side.

"How?"

"I shan't tell you how, because I want me to be the person who gives it to you."

"Why?"

"Because it's going to be a prize."

"What for?"

"Ballet. If I could promise you pocket money,

would you work properly at ballet like Madame Raine made you?"

They were standing on a path. Hilary scratched up some gravel with her toe.

"It's so boring, all that barre. Musical comedy, tap and acrobatics are much more fun."

"But if you could be a proper ballerina, you'd like that better, you know you would."

"I wouldn't mind if I could just be one, it's learning to be one I hate."

"But you wouldn't mind the learning so much if you had pocket money."

Hilary thought of her morning classes, of Pat saying "Straighten that supporting leg, Hilary." "Hilary, turn out that thigh." Of endless pliés, ronds de jambes, battements frappés, and all the rest of the exercises. Then she thought of eating a coffee whirl, and of a little rabbit, perhaps made of velvet, and they won.

"All right. I'll work. How much pocket money?"

"I don't know," said Rachel. "I'll tell you directly I do."

Rachel knocked on the studio door, and was glad to hear Uncle Tom shout "come in." He was painting the sort of picture he liked painting, or rather he had painted it, and was now doing finishing things to it. He looked pleased to see Rachel.

"Hullo, my dear. Come in."

It seemed to Rachel rude to ask about pocket money straight away, so she had a look at the picture. It was even odder than the park one. At first Rachel thought it was just a sort of colored pattern, then it began to divide up and she saw shapes that were meant to be people dancing. In the background, what she had thought was a black and white pattern became a Negro band.

"Is it a party?" she asked.

Uncle Tom held up his thumb and, shutting one eye, stared across it at his picture.

"Sort of, it's a dance club."

Now that Rachel could see that the shapes were people she noticed they were dancing in a very gay way.

"Would you call that musical comedy dancing?"

Uncle Tom put his arm round her.

"Rougher than that. How's your dancing getting on?"

Rachel liked the feel of his arm, and she leaned against him.

"I'll never make a dancer. Quite truthfully, I'm not cut out for it. But I'm better than I was."

Uncle Tom hugged her to him.

"Poor old lady. How's Hilary doing?"

Rachel pulled away from him.

"It's her I came to see you about. You remember

you said you couldn't interfere about her dancing."
He nodded.

"I did and I meant it. I can't."

Rachel looked up at him earnestly.

"But do you think you could about pocket money? I mean, could you arrange that I had a little of the money I'll have when I grow up, each week?"

Uncle Tom sat down in a big armchair and pulled her on to his knee.

"I'm sure I could. But I can see there's something behind that question. What is it?"

Out came the whole story. It had been bottled up in Rachel so long it was rather like water coming with a burst out of a tap that has been stopped up. About Hilary's mother having been a dancer. The teacher who had taken Hilary to Madame Raine. How Madame Raine had given Hilary a half-hour lesson every day for nothing. How she had said her reward would be seeing Hilary dance at Covent Garden. How her mother had said however poor they were the one thing they would never give up was Hilary's ballet lessons. The last bit was difficult to tell anyone.

"The doctor who looked after Mummie said she sent me a message. It was that I was to see Hilary went on with dancing lessons."

Uncle Tom played gently with one of Rachel's plaits.

"I expect I'm a silly old uncle, but surely Hilary is learning to dance."

Rachel struggled to find simple words to make him see.

"Acrobatics, musical comedy, and tap aren't the sort of dancing Mummie meant. But she does have proper ballet lessons too, every day. Really proper ones. I watched once."

Uncle Tom was puzzled.

"One ballet lesson isn't enough?"

"It's not that, it's Hilary. She doesn't bother with ballet much. She likes tap, acrobatics and musical comedy better. But she wants pocket money, and if I had some I could bribe her to work at ballet."

Uncle Tom understood at last.

"So that's it. I don't know anything about ballet, but if I were you I wouldn't forget the proverb 'You can lead a horse to water but you cannot make him drink.'"

Rachel would not listen.

"Hilary's got to be a ballerina, absolutely got to! Mummie wanted her to be one."

Uncle Tom saw that he could not talk Rachel out of believing it was her duty to plan for Hilary.

"Have it your own way. How much pocket money do you want?"

"I think, from what Hilary said, that some of the

Wonders get a great deal . . . as much perhaps as two-and-sixpence a week."

"Is that all? I'm not a rich man, but I can manage that much. What about you? You'll want pocket money too."

"No, thank you, not at present anyway, and Hilary's will have to be a secret."

Uncle Tom understood that.

"Of course. Now, here's the arrangement. I'll give you secretly half-a-crown each Saturday, which you can pass on to Hilary if she works. If you want any extra money for yourself you'll come and ask for it. How's that?"

Rachel flung her arms around his neck.

"Thank you. You're a most gorgeously understanding person."

11

SUMMER TERM

The pocket money idea was a good one. Nothing could make Hilary into a hard worker, but for her she worked hard, and so of course her ballet dancing improved. But, though Rachel did not know it, so were her acrobatics, tap and musical comedy dancing improving. And Hilary was working hard at these, not for pocket money but because to her learning that sort of dancing was not only fun but could lead to an ambition she was hiding from Rachel. It was to join a troupe the moment she was old enough to have a license.

That summer three troupes were working. Hilary and Rachel were looking out of their bedroom window when the twenty-six Wonders who were going to Blackpool—twenty-four dancers and two under-studies—got into the coach that was driving them to the station.

"Lucky beasts," said Hilary. "I wish it was me."

Rachel was looking at the Blackpool Wonders with horror. She turned a shocked face to Hilary.

"You couldn't want to be one of them, you couldn't!"

Hilary secretly thought the Wonders looked rather nice. The little-girl frocks were pale blue, over their arms they each carried a bright blue summer over-coat, and on each head was the sort of white cap American sailors wear, with the initials "W.W." on the front of them.

"It's more fun being them than being us. I'd like to go to Blackpool."

Rachel spoke fiercely.

"You mustn't think like that, ever, ever, ever. You're going to dance at Covent Garden."

Hilary looked wistfully at the bus. The last of the Wonders had climbed in and the conductor was shutting the door.

"Anyway I wish I was twelve, and old enough to have a license. I hate doing nothing but learn."

Dulcie, standing by the front door beside her mother, and waving a condescending good-by to the Wonders and their matrons, was saying much the same things as Hilary.

"Oh, Mum, I wish I was twelve and going with them."

Mrs. Wintle was as shocked as Rachel had been.

"I quite understand you wanting to be twelve, but mother's girl won't be joining any troupe. Mum has bigger ideas than that for her."

"Will I be dressed as a Wonder?"

What Dulcie would wear when she was a Wonder was something about which Mrs. Wintle had thought quite a lot. Dressing all the children alike was a splendid advertisement, but should Dulcie be dressed like the others? Wouldn't it suggest she was just one of the school, instead of a brilliant little star in the making?

"Mum hasn't decided that yet, darling. Perhaps something like the others, so that it shows you belong to the school. But a rather special little girl must have rather special clothes, don't you think?"

Dulcie had a faint feeling of jealousy for Hilary.

Ballet was only a side line, but it was annoying that somebody younger than she was should be ahead of her at any form of dancing. And it was no good pretending Hilary was not ahead of her at ballet, for Hilary was wearing block shoes, which Pat said she would not be ready for until the autumn.

"Will Hilary wear something special too, if she gets solos?"

Mrs. Wintle had not made up her mind about Hilary either. Of course it would be nice for the school if Hilary's dancing was good enough to get her a principal part, but on the other hand she didn't want any child stealing the limelight from Dulcie.

"There's no need to think about that yet. Hilary will start in a troupe, which Mum's own girlie will not."

Dulcie giggled.

"Imagine when Rachel's twelve! Think of her in one of those white hats. Won't she look funny, Mum?"

Mrs. Wintle thought of Rachel's pale face, odd-looking high cheekbones and ugly plaits. It was, to her, an unattractive picture.

"I will have to do something about her before then. She won't be twelve for a year and a half. Perhaps her hair would look better permed. Or I might bleach it —fair hair can be striking with brown eyes—but she's the most unattractive child I ever trained."

Mrs. Storm did not think Rachel the most unattractive child she had ever taught. In fact, as the summer term passed, she found she began to admire her.

"It's such an unusual little face," she told her husband. "She's got more color now, and lost the spots she had when she came to me, and when she's interested she lights up all over."

Mrs. Storm was the only teacher in the school who had a chance to see Rachel lighting up all over. Rachel liked both Pat and Ena, and did her best to work well for them, but it is difficult to look happy when you are thinking hard about something you do not like doing.

There was no anxious frown to spoil the Rachel Mrs. Storm saw, for she liked lessons and really loved the acting classes, which was more than could be said for Dulcie or Hilary.

To Hilary learning anything by heart was work which she detested. Dulcie did not mind learning words by heart, in fact it was no trouble to her. But her acting classes were a labor because her way of saying anything out loud was the exact opposite of how Mrs. Storm thought she ought to sound. Hilary, who though she was slow at learning words was good at making them up, made the girls in Group Two roll about with laughter when she imitated Dulcie. Mrs. Storm was teaching the children scenes from

Alice in Wonderland and *A Midsummer Night's Dream.*

"Here's Dulcie," Hilary would say, "first being Alice talking to the caterpillar, and then being the caterpillar talking to Alice, then being Puck. 'Who are you?' the caterpillar says. Then Dulcie steps forward like this, as if she was going to dance a solo, and says in her fancy-ish way: 'I don't know, not just at present. I know who I was when I got up this morning, but I've changed lots of times since then.' "

"Now this is her being the caterpillar. 'What d'you mean by that, explain yourself.' "

"Then this is her being Puck. 'What hempen homespuns have we swaggering here, so near the cradle of our fairy queen? What, a play going on? I'll be an auditor, an actor too perhaps, if I see cause.' "

Although Hilary got some of the words wrong, it was no wonder the girls laughed, for though Hilary exaggerated Dulcie, she did sound like her, and made Dulcie say all the parts exactly alike. The truth was that since she was a baby Dulcie had been brought up to know she was a very clever, unusual little girl. And because this was what she thought, it came out in her voice, which, though Hilary called it fancy-ish, Pat and Ena described as affected, and Mrs. Storm as dreadful.

It was on a day when they were working at *A Mid-*

summer Night's Dream that Mrs. Storm had an idea. They were acting the scene in the wood, where Oberon and Titania quarrel. Hilary was Puck, Mrs. Storm read the fairy, Dulcie was Oberon and Rachel Titania. Hilary made rather a nice Puck, and Mrs. Storm, who loved Shakespeare, settled back happily to enjoy the rest of the scene. But Dulcie's first words sent shivers down her spine. There was no attempt at a proud fairy king, just the usual Dulcie saying in her rather high, pleased-with-yourself voice: " 'Ill met by moonlight, proud Titania.' "

Mrs. Storm was going to stop the scene and take Dulcie through her lines again when she found she had ceased being aggravated by Dulcie and was instead really listening to and enjoying Rachel. Of course Rachel was only a little girl reciting verse, but—and this was what suddenly struck Mrs. Storm—she could speak verse keeping both the sense and the rhythm, and she could forget she was Rachel. "She's enjoying herself, bless her," she thought. "And if she enjoys it, why shouldn't she have more of it?"

When the moment came for Titania to sweep off the stage, followed by her fairies, and before the scene between Puck and Oberon, Mrs. Storm said:

"That was very nice indeed, Rachel. You almost persuaded me the schoolroom was gone, and that we were in a wood near Athens."

Dulcie did not like that.

"You seem to forget that half the scene was me being Oberon."

Mrs. Storm wanted to say "The scene was half you all right, though there was no Oberon." But it was a waste of time, for Dulcie would not understand what she meant. So instead she said:

"No, I didn't forget, but Rachel was the one who made me feel I was in a fairy wood. Now let's see if you and Hilary can give me the same feeling."

After lessons Mrs. Storm told Rachel to wait behind. When the door had closed behind the other two, she said:

"I was thinking that as you like acting it would be a good idea if you learned extra elocution for me while the other two are dancing in the mornings. I think, if I tried, I might manage to get in by ten, and work at the parts with you."

Mrs. Storm did not say that learning extra parts in the mornings was a secret between her and Rachel, but somehow it became one. Rachel did tell Hilary, but Hilary only said:

"Oh, my goodness, how awful for you. I wouldn't wonder if she made you learn that awful Rosalind or one of those." Then she forgot that Rachel had told her.

Learning extra elocution was not the sort of thing

you talked to Pursey about. Food, clothes and the children she had been nurse to were Pursey's subjects. But Rachel did say to her at one of their after-lunch talks:

"I'm learning the 'Make-me-a-willow-cabin' speech as homework."

But Pursey only answered:

"And very nice I'm sure, my lambkin, and talking of making, I'll have to be cutting out a new ballet tunic for Hilary, that pink one she brought from Folkestone is a rag."

Pat and Ena never thought of anything but dancing, and Wanda and Yolanta were not interested in what the children learned. Rachel never spoke to Aunt Cora if she could help it, so that only left Uncle Tom. Actually he would have been interested, but Rachel did not know that, and in her busy life she hardly saw him. So quite by accident the extra elocution was a secret, and, though neither Mrs. Storm nor Rachel guessed it, a very important one.

12

SUMMER HOLIDAYS' PLANS

It was Mrs. Wintle's custom during the summer holidays to visit the towns where her Wonders were performing. Naturally Dulcie went too, and so did Pursey. Sometimes Uncle Tom started with them, but he usually left them to wander off alone with his sketch book. That summer, of course, there were

Rachel and Hilary to be thought about. Dulcie was the first to speak about them.

"Mum," she asked one morning, after her dancing lesson, "do Rachel and Hilary have to come with us when we go away?"

Mrs. Wintle had been puzzling over the same problem. She knew, because they had written to say so when Rachel and Hilary had first come to live with her, that both the doctor and Madame Raine would like the children to stay with them at Folkestone. But she was not sure it would be a good idea. She had got Hilary training as a Little Wonder, and she did not want that silly talk about The Royal Ballet School starting again. But she had been thinking of writing to the doctor to ask if he would like to have Rachel to stay for a week or two.

"I expect we'll take Hilary. It'll be nice for you to have her to do things with."

As her mother said those words Dulcie realized for the first time how much she would hate it. It was bad enough having to share a governess and walks in term time, but at least she did have her own room, and usually managed to sit at a different table from the one Rachel and Hilary sat at for meals. But if in the holidays only Hilary came she would have to do everything with her, perhaps even share a bedroom. Besides, it would spoil her grandness. Always before she had been the great Mrs. Wintle's little Dulcie, visiting the working Wonders, and, as she thought, pleasing them by copying her mother and saying something kind to each one. If she could have seen the Wonders prancing around after she had left, imitating what they called "Dulcie-Pulsie doing her stuff," her cheeks would have burned. But, not knowing what the Wonders thought of her, she could only imagine her condescending tours of theater dressing rooms, and her meetings with the Wonders on sea fronts and beaches being spoiled because Hilary was there to share her glory.

"Oh Mum, must she come? Can't we be just us like we usually are?"

Mrs. Wintle wished too they could be just themselves, but she was not risking Hilary meeting Madame Raine again.

"Mum knows just how you feel, but rather special little girls must behave in rather a special way, and that means being kind to other children who are not so clever or lucky as she is."

"But why must it be only Hilary? If Rachel comes too they can do things together, and not bother us."

This was a new idea to Mrs. Wintle, who had only thought it would be nice to be rid of Rachel for a week or two.

"All right, pet-ums," she said, glad she had not yet

written to the doctor. "Rachel shall come too, if that's what Mum's girlie would like."

That same morning Mrs. Wintle went to the wardrobe.

"We're taking Rachel and Hilary with us when we go on tour, Pursey. I had thought of sending Rachel to a doctor they knew at Folkestone, but Dulcie thinks having both with us will be less trouble than having Hilary only, so that's that."

Pursey strongly disapproved of the decision being left to Dulcie, but this time she had to agree with her, if for a different reason.

"I must say I don't think the little girls should be separated. I never believed in special treatment for one and not the other."

Mrs. Wintle thought Pursey was talking nonsense.

"It might have done Rachel good to be packed off to Folkestone while Hilary toured with us. She must learn that jealousy doesn't pay. However, I can't have poor little Dulcie's holiday spoilt, so if she wants her cousins she must have them. Now, what about the children's clothes? They'll need some new things. Come with me to their bedroom, and show me what they have."

Throughout the summer term, by letting down and letting out, Pursey had made Rachel's and Hilary's last summer frocks do.

"They're a bit short on you," she had said in her cozy voice to Rachel, "but so beautifully made it's a shame not to finish them out. Besides, you're in your dancing things most of the day."

Last year's frocks, however beautifully made, were not Mrs. Wintle's idea of how nieces of hers should be dressed when they were touring with her. But she had not built up a successful business by being wasteful, so now she studied each frock as Pursey held it up, and decided what was to be done with it. At last Pursey held up the marigold frock.

"This is in lovely condition, and ever so nice a color, but it won't let out any more."

As Mrs. Wintle took the frock from Pursey she remembered she had seen it before.

"Rachel was wearing this the first time I saw her. What a sight she looked!" She turned the dress around, making a face at it.

Rachel had come to her morning lessons without a handkerchief and had been given permission by Mrs. Storm to run up and fetch one. She had not heard voices in the bedroom, so she ran straight into the room just at the moment her aunt was looking at the frock. Pursey saw Rachel, but Mrs. Wintle did not, so she went on saying what she had been going to say.

"Extraordinary taste my sister-in-law had. Imagine this color on a sallow child like Rachel," she said, tossing the frock in a despising way to Pursey. "Cut it up, Pursey. It will make a pair of shorts for Hilary."

Before her aunt could say another word Rachel, two flaming spots of color in her cheeks, and her face screwed up with what looked like bad temper, but was really her way of trying not to cry, had snatched the marigold frock from Pursey. Then, as if it could feel it had been insulted, she hugged it to her.

"Don't you dare touch this frock, Aunt Cora! It's mine. I won't have it cut up into shorts for Hilary."

Pursey made tch-tch-ing sounds.

"Now, now Rachel, there's no need to carry on. Your Auntie is only doing what's best for you . . ."

Rachel flung around and faced her.

"She's not, Pursey, she's not! How dare she say Hilary is to have shorts made out of my frock?"

Mrs. Wintle gave Pursey a what-did-I-tell-you look. Then she turned to Rachel.

"While I am in charge of you it is my decision what clothes you wear. I realize you are jealous of Hilary, but I am not going to allow that to influence me. No matter what fuss you make she is your adopted sister, and will be treated in every way as you are treated." Rachel opened her mouth to explain, but her aunt stopped her. "Not another word. I am disgusted with you."

Rachel just held out until the door shut behind

Aunt Cora. Then, tears streaming down her cheeks, she flung herself at Pursey.

"It was Mummie's favorite frock. I'm not jealous of Hilary, truly I'm not. But she can't say in that sneery voice 'cut it up.' Not Mummie's favorite frock, she can't."

Pursey sat down and pulled Rachel onto her lap. Then, as if she was a baby, she rocked her to and fro.

"I know you're not jealous, my lambkin. Pursey has learned that. But you acted very foolish. Your auntie is taking you and Hilary away with her, and was planning new frocks and all. She meant no harm saying the orange dress would cut into shorts. She wasn't to know you were so fond of it."

Rachel tried to speak through her sobs.

"But she said Mummie had ex . . . extraordinary taste. She hadn't, she'd gorgeous taste."

Pursey's voice became cozier than ever.

"Of course she had. Lovely frocks she made you, I never saw prettier. But you know you shouldn't have spoken to your auntie the way you did. You said to me the first morning you were here: 'You won't throw anything away, will you?' And I said of course I wouldn't. What an idea!"

"But this isn't throwing away."

Pursey hugged Rachel to her.

"Same thing. You should trust old Pursey. Nothing

wasn't going to be touched or given away, not unless you said so."

"But now the marigold dress has got to be shorts for Hilary."

Pursey patted Rachel's arm.

"Hilary has to have a pair of shorts that color, but what's the matter with me buying a piece to match? That marigold frock is going back in your drawer, and there it will stay until you tell Pursey what to do with it."

13

LIFE WITH THE WONDERS

In spite of it beginning badly because of the fuss about the marigold frock, Rachel quite enjoyed the summer holiday, and Hilary loved every minute of it. Pursey bought some marigold-colored linen and made Hilary's shorts.

"There," she said, showing them to Rachel, "nobody could swear those weren't your frock once, and what I say is what you don't know you can't grieve about."

The first town they visited was Cardiff, where the touring Wonders were dancing in a revue called *Look up and Smile*. The first evening they were in Cardiff all the party, except Uncle Tom, who said he would rather go for a walk, went to see the revue. It was the sort where the funny man has a great deal to do in a very noisy way, and as well has to smash things and throw messes like whitewash at people. There was a leading lady with very gold hair who sang songs, lots of less important people, and a grown-up chorus. The Wonders had quite a lot to do, so they had been picked from the number one group. But they were either too tall, too fat, or too plain for the best shows. All the same, all twelve of the troupe were clever, and the manager of *Look up and Smile* came to the free box he had given to Mrs. Wintle and told her so.

"They're just the ticket, Mrs. W. Really smart kiddies, ever so popular wherever we go."

The manager might think the troupe smart, but Mrs. Wintle found a lot that was wrong with them. She sat in the front of the box looking grand, and writing down on a pad anything she did not like.

"Poor beasts," Hilary whispered to Rachel, nodding at the Wonders, "they can see she's writing things about them."

Faults that Mrs. Wintle missed were pointed out by Dulcie.

"Barbara muddled that leg over, didn't she, Mum? Did you see Susan's feet? I don't think Mary ought to turn a cartwheel if she can't do it, do you, Mum? Ooh, Mum, have you put down to tell Rona about her tap? She was right off the beat."

Pursey tried to help the Wonders, murmuring in her cozy way each time Dulcie spoke:

"I think they're ever so clever," or "I think they're doing wonderfully."

But Pursey might just as well not have spoken for all the attention paid to her.

"Don't be silly, Pursey," was all Mrs. Wintle said. "You keep your eye on the clothes. You know nothing about dancing."

Rachel, who by now knew a little about dancing, was impressed by the Wonders, even though she did not admire what they had to do.

"I can't see what Dulcie thinks they are doing wrong," she whispered to Hilary.

Hilary had greater knowledge.

"I can," she whispered back, "but I think Dulcie is an absolute toad to make Aunt Cora see things she hasn't noticed."

After the show they all went backstage to visit the Wonders. Rachel and Hilary were terribly embarrassed, for Mrs. Wintle behaved as if she thought she and Dulcie were royal.

"Well done, chickabiddies," said Mrs. Wintle. "We were proud of you, weren't we, Dulcie?"

Dulcie managed by turning her head to include all twelve Wonders in a kindly smile.

"I thought you did awfully well."

"But," Mrs. Wintle went on, "there are of course some little slacknesses here and there. So rehearsal tomorrow at ten. Good night, dears." She turned to the head matron and her assistant. "Have they been good children?"

The matron and her assistant had become very fond of the Wonders, but even had they not been, they would not have told Mrs. Wintle tales about them.

"They have behaved splendidly. Not one of them has missed a day at school, and they've all been obedient and helpful in the lodgings, and very good on the train journeys, which, as you know, have frequently been both long and tiring."

Mrs. Wintle nodded.

"Just what I expect to hear about my Wonders. We're all proud of our W.W., aren't we, chickabiddies? Good night."

Dulcie gave another smile which took in everybody.

"Good night. I think I'll come and watch your rehearsal."

"Good night, dears," said Pursey. "I thought you were ever so good."

Mrs. Wintle looked at Rachel and Hilary.

"Say good night to the children."

Rachel licked her lips. She thought she knew exactly how the Wonders felt and was sure they must be hating her and Hilary.

"Good night," she whispered, "and thank you."

Hilary too was certain what the Wonders were thinking, but it did not embarrass her. She stepped forward to let Mrs. Wintle and Dulcie pass her, which meant the Wonders could see her face, and they could not.

"Good night," she said. Then she winked.

The Cardiff week passed quickly. Every day after the rehearsal with Mrs. Wintle was over the matrons took the Wonders and their understudy out by bus to places of interest, or along the coast to the beach, and Hilary went with them. Rachel could have gone too, but she felt stiff and awkward with the Wonders. She was delighted when, the second morning, Uncle Tom asked her to go sketching with him.

Hilary found life with the Wonders as much fun as she had heard it would be. Because it was their profession, whenever there was a flat place on which to work, everybody tried to turn cartwheels and somer-saults or to walk on their hands. Hilary was delighted to find that her acrobatics were coming along so well that she was nearly up to the standard of the other girls.

As well as practicing acrobatics with the Wonders, Hilary found it was grand having thirteen girls to talk to, all of whom liked the sort of things she liked. They all laughed every day until they rolled about, imitating Dulcie.

"Here's Dulcie-Pulsie dancing a hornpipe." "Watch me, this is Dulcie-Pulsie doing her stuff to the theater manager."

Nearly all the troupe were north London girls, coming from back streets and overcrowded homes, so to them the tour was a treat from start to finish. They had such fun it was no wonder that, as each day passed, Hilary was more and more sure that the life of a troupe dancer was the life for her.

"But you could do better than us," a girl called Anne, whom Hilary particularly liked, pointed out to her. "You've had proper training in ballet. If you work you might get principal parts."

"I don't want principal parts," Hilary explained. "It wasn't me that asked to learn ballet, it was a teacher at my school at Folkestone who thought I ought to. Since I've been living with Rachel's Aunt Cora I know I'd much rather do your sort of dancing, and best of all acrobatics."

"But you're working hard at ballet, aren't you?" Anne asked. "Pursey says that Pat says you're the best at ballet in the school."

Rachel was not around, but all the same Hilary lowered her voice.

"It's Rachel who wants me to do ballet."

"Why?"

Hilary shrugged her shoulders.

"She thinks her mother wanted me to, but I don't think she minded. I think she thought my mother was a dancer, so I ought to be one too. Well, I'm going to be one, but not The Royal Ballet School sort, just a Wonder."

"I should explain that to Rachel, if I was you," said Anne.

Hilary got so close to Anne she could whisper.

"Will you swear not to tell anybody, if I tell you something?"

At Mrs. Wintle's school swearing not to tell something was always done the same way. Anne raised a hand.

"I swear on my awkward-Adas."

"Well, I have to work at ballet because if I do Rachel gets me pocket money. I think her Uncle Tom gives it to her. But, in a year and a half when I'm twelve and can earn money, I'm never going to do ballet again, never, never, never."

After Cardiff the family moved to Blackpool, where they stayed for two weeks, and then to the east coast, where the troupe of Wonders were working in a holiday camp. In each place the routine was the same: the visit to the show, with Mrs. Wintle taking notes, the royal tour of the dressing room, the rehearsal the next morning. Neither the Blackpool Wonders nor the holiday camp Wonders had as much to do as the *Look up and Smile* Wonders. But Hilary found them all equally friendly, and as much fun, and they all spent their spare time the same way, mostly working at acrobatics. With all three troupes Hilary was very popular, for she had a way of saying things that made the other girls laugh. Besides, they thought she was gloriously unsnobbish, seeing she was a sort of niece of Mrs. Wintle's, and had been meant to go to The Royal Ballet School.

The Wonders quite liked Rachel, but they did not see much of her, for almost every day she went off early with Uncle Tom and often did not get back before the Wonders had left for the theatre. To begin with Uncle Tom tried to persuade Rachel to sketch, and offered to teach her, but he soon gave up because he found what she really liked was reading. Uncle

Tom was fond of reading too, and almost every day bought Rachel a book. As well she had one of the boy's speeches from *Henry V* and *The Princess and the Pea* to study, for she was learning them for Mrs. Storm for her special elocution class. Often Uncle Tom would look up from his painting and watch Rachel in a pleased sort of way.

"I'm glad you're such a reader, old lady. Your father and I had read almost every book in the children's branch of our public library by the time we were in double figures. There's nothing like getting the reading habit. It will be a great help to you when you are twelve, especially if you tour, for those long railway journeys on Sundays must be an almighty bore."

Rachel was reading *The Wind in the Willows*. She left Ratty and Mole and thought of reading in trains.

"When I'm old enough for a license I should think, if I go on tour, the railway journeys would be the best part. The time in the theater will be the worst."

Uncle Tom bent down and gave Rachel's plaits an affectionate pull.

"I wouldn't start worrying yet, a lot of water has got to go under the bridge before you'll be twelve." He broke off, his artist's eye caught by what he saw. "You ought to wear those plaits on the top of your head, old lady, not sticking out at each side." He pulled Rachel to her feet, and crossed her plaits over. "They suit you like that."

Rachel remembered her mother saying exactly the same thing. She pulled away from Uncle Tom, looking cross as she always did when something made her unhappy.

"I can't fix them myself, but I used to wear them like that."

Uncle Tom knew Rachel by now. He went back to his painting.

"I expect Pursey could fix them, I'll have a word with her. In the meantime, I'm starving, how would my niece feel about laying out the lunch?"

While they visited the holiday camp Wonders, Aunt Cora, Uncle Tom and Dulcie lived in a grand hotel, but Rachel, Hilary and Pursey lived in chalets. Pursey had a big double one all to herself, for she had the Wonders' apple blossom dresses to do up, and needed room to work. Rachel and Hilary had the chalet next to her, so it was quite easy for Pursey to do Rachel's hair, and a great improvement it was. The Wonders were the first people to notice the change.

"My goodness, Rachel, I do like your hair done like that."

"Look at Rachel. It ought to be you, not Hilary, who's good at ballet, because you look like a ballet dancer."

"Fancy," said one of the matrons, "I wouldn't have thought just pinning up plaits could make such a difference. You'll be a very distinguished-looking Wonder when the time comes, Rachel."

These compliments made Rachel embarrassed and self-conscious, so she went back to her chalet after breakfast, meaning to let her plaits loose again before Aunt Cora saw her. But Hilary would not let her touch her hair.

"Let her see you. She's always so sneery to you, and so proud of Dulcie-Pulsie, it'll do her good to see you can look pretty too."

As it happened Aunt Cora, when Rachel met her, was so full of a plan for Dulcie that she never glanced at Rachel, but hurried past her into Pursey's chalet.

"On Saturday week there's a talent competition, Pursey. I am entering Dulcie for it. Now I want you to make her something pretty to wear."

"If there's a talent competition," said Pursey, "why not enter Hilary too? Nice advertisement if we could walk off with two prizes."

Mrs. Wintle had thought somebody might suggest that, and was ready with an answer.

"No, Hilary hasn't learned long enough with me. As I'm always telling you, Pursey, it's easy to strain a child if she works too hard before she's got into my ways. Now about Dulcie's dress. I thought a crimson taffeta can-can frock, with rows of little frills inside the skirt, would be sweet on her."

After Mrs. Wintle had gone, Pursey, muttering to herself at the thought of all the work there was in a can-can frock, sent Rachel to fetch Dulcie to be measured.

"A pity, though," she said, "that I'm not telling you to fetch Hilary too. To my mind she's got as good a chance in a talent contest as Dulcie has."

Rachel was just moving when Pursey said that; it stopped her dead.

"Oh, Pursey, darling angel Pursey, please, please don't say that to anyone but me. Hilary mustn't do high kicks in a can-can dress, truly she mustn't."

Pursey shook her head.

"You are a funny one, always on about Hilary's dancing. But don't worry, she's not wearing a can-can dress nor anything else, for your Auntie won't let her enter for the competition, so that's that."

But it was not that, for Mrs. Wintle had not reckoned on her Wonders. It all started when they and Hilary, after practicing their acrobatics, were standing round a show case in which were displayed the prizes for the talent competition. The first prize for the girls was a gold wrist watch.

"Isn't it beautiful?" one of the Wonders said. "Whoever wins it will be ever so lucky."

Hilary thought a gold wrist watch was the grandest possession a child could have.

"It'll be Dulcie."

"Dulcie!" said all the Wonders. "Is she going in for it?"

Hilary had heard from Rachel about the can-can dress, so she told the Wonders what she knew.

"And she's so terribly good no one here could beat her, and the awful thing is she's already got one wrist watch."

The idea struck all the Wonders at once.

"I know someone who could beat her," said the troupe leader who was called Poppy, "it's you."

Hilary gasped.

"Me! But I'm not entered, and I've nothing to wear."

"I'll see to that," said Poppy. "And we'll all rehearse you and rehearse you until you drop. But it's a secret, mind. We must all swear not to tell anybody."

Each of the Wonders and Hilary raised a hand.

"I swear on my awkward-Adas."

"Oh goodness," said Poppy when the swearing was over, "if only you could win, Hilary. I think if I could see you beat Dulcie-Pulsie I would be happy forever and ever."

14

THE TALENT CONTEST

The talent contest took three days. The grand finale
was to be at six o'clock on a Saturday evening in front
of all the campers, when the finalists in each class
would perform. There had been two or three talent
competitions for children, so the Wonders knew just
how they worked, though of course they themselves

could not enter as they were professionals. Because several of the entrants might share the same surname every child was given a number, and it was by their numbers they were called when it was their turn to perform.

The Wonders knew the woman who ran the competitions, so Poppy went to her and entered Hilary. The woman wrote down Hilary Lennox, aged ten, and told Poppy her friend would be number forty-seven. It did not strike her as odd that Hilary had been entered by Poppy, for she had asked all the Wonders to keep an eye open for talent in the camp. In any case, it was quite usual for parents, aunts or friends to enter children.

Once Hilary had become number forty-seven the question was what she was to do, and where was she to rehearse.

"If you're to beat Dulcie," Poppy said, "you ought to dance on your pointes, for she's better than you at other sorts of dancing."

Hilary turned a cartwheel.

"I know, and for that gorgeous watch I'd even do that. But I haven't my shoes with me, and if I had I don't know a dance to do, and I couldn't make one up."

Poppy turned to the other Wonders for suggestions. "Any ideas?"

It was the understudy, Alice, who answered. She was a clever child, the best dancer in the troupe, but she was tall, and to be tall was a fatal fault in a Wonder. At best it made you a permanent understudy, at worst it meant Mrs. Wintle ceased to employ you.

"As Hilary can't dance on her pointes her only hope of beating Dulcie is to be funny."

"What sort of funny?" asked Hilary.

"Just what you always do when you're talking about Dulcie." She turned to the Wonders. "You know what I mean."

"But Mrs. Wintle will be there," said Poppy. "Hilary couldn't be Dulcie in front of her."

"But she needn't be Dulcie," Alice explained. "She could be just any awful child."

Hilary saw what Alice meant, and was charmed by her idea.

"I'll do a Dulcie day. Her getting up, doing lessons, going for a walk, eating, and going to bed. It'll be a very primsy sort of dance, like Dulcie is, but I'll do cartwheels and walking on my hands as well because I like those."

Poppy looked worried.

"What on earth shall she wear?"

Alice was still full of ideas.

"Why not one of our uniform frocks? Our mothers

pay for those, so no one can say we shouldn't lend them."

Hilary was enchanted.

"One of those little-girl frocks? It'll be exactly right. Has anyone got a clean one they could lend?"

Alice pointed to the smallest Wonder.

"She must wear yours, Betty. It ought to fit, but if it needs altering I'll do it while you're all on the stage."

"But what," said Poppy, "will she do about music?"

Alice had even thought of that.

"Mr. Pinkerton. He's awfully nice. I bet he'd help."

Pinkie Pinkerton conducted the theater orchestra. He had just finished running through a new song when he saw the Wonders sitting at the back of the theater.

"Hullo, kiddies," he called out. "Mrs. W. taking another rehearsal this morning?"

Poppy left her seat and joined him.

"No. But could you possibly spare us a few minutes? We want your help."

Pinkie Pinkerton was a good-natured man, with children of his own. He dismissed his band and went to the back of the theater and joined the Wonders.

"Now what is it? What mess have you got yourselves into?"

Pinkie Pinkerton saw no reason why Hilary should

not enter for the talent competition. And if she wanted to keep it secret that she was entering he saw no reason why she should not. As well, when he saw the sort of number Hilary was planning to do, he found it rather fun arranging her music. He linked together old nursery rhyme tunes, starting with "Girls and Boys Come Out to Play" and finishing with "Rockaby Baby," but he jazzed them up or, as Hilary said, made them Dulcie-ish.

But even with all this arranged, getting Hilary ready by the following Thursday to take part in the first round of the contest was terribly difficult. Pinkie Pinkerton could not have been kinder, but proper rehearsals were so hard to arrange. To begin with the Wonders were not allowed in the theater without a matron, and they would have got into trouble if they had been caught asking Mr. Pinkerton to help. Then it was difficult to have a rehearsal on the stage without anyone noticing it was going on. But on Sunday night, after the camp evening service at which his band had been playing, Pinkie Pinkerton found some of the Wonders and told them he thought he had everything fixed. Nobody used the ballroom at seven in the morning except cleaners, and they wouldn't talk. So if the Wonders could get a matron to bring Hilary along then she could get a good hour's rehearsal undisturbed.

When Hilary heard the news she knew at once who would help her. Before she went to bed that night she slipped into Pursey's chalet.

"Pursey angel, I want your help, but you must swear not to tell anybody, especially Rachel."

Pursey heard what was planned in silence. Then, when Hilary had finished telling her, she gave one of her warm purry Pursey-ish chuckles.

"Bless the child, whatever will you and the Wonders think of next! Still, I was always an early riser, so I reckon seven in the morning won't hurt me for a day or two." Then she paused, and slowly a worried look came on her face. "But I don't like deceit. I wish you could tell your Auntie what's planned, but I can see you can't. But couldn't you let Rachel know? You're her sister in a manner of speaking and she's ever so fond of you."

Pursey was sitting on her bed, and Hilary in one jump was kneeling beside her.

"Silly, silly Pursey. Of course Rachel's fond of me, just as I'm fondest of her of anybody in the world. But she's so odd about the sort of dancing I'm going to do. She thinks I ought to do nothing but ballet."

Pursey put an arm round Hilary.

"I know, dear, and I suppose she has her reasons, but I must say I've never understood what they are.

It's just that I never have liked anything under-handed among my children."

Hilary hugged Pursey.

"It isn't underhanded really, it's just that Rachel doesn't know about dancing. So you will come at seven, won't you, Pursey? Promise?"

Pursey kissed her good night.

"I promise. Now run off to bed or you'll never be fit to dance at seven in the morning. And no lies to Rachel, mind. Tell her the truth, that you're getting up early to dance with the Wonders."

"I'll call it playing with the Wonders," said Hilary. "I never talk dancing to Rachel. Good night, Pursey, you're an angel."

When the talent contest started on Thursday the children who were taking part were called in groups to the theater. Poppy had figured out that the chance of Hilary and Dulcie being called at the same time was so unlikely that they need not worry about it. She was quite right, for Dulcie was called on Thursday morning and Hilary on Friday afternoon. For the finals there were to be outside judges, but for the preliminary rounds the professional dancers who taught ballroom dancing to the campers and the producer of the camp show were the judges. Mrs. Wintle would have been asked to join them but, of course, as Dulcie was competing, she could not. The Wonders had early news of the time at which Dulcie would dance.

"You're all to be in the theater at ten sharp tomorrow morning," said the head matron after the Wednesday matinée. "Dulcie is doing a dance in the talent contest, and Mrs. Wintle thinks you should watch her." The Wonders made noises as if they were being sick, for which the matron had to scold them. "That's enough of that. She's a very clever little dancer, and you can all learn something from watching her."

The maddening thing was that it was perfectly true Dulcie was a clever dancer, and that the Wonders could all learn something from watching her. She looked charming in her can-can dress and sailed through her contest with almost full marks.

"What a delicious child," the Wonders heard the female ballroom dancer say. "I can't imagine anyone will beat her."

Gloomily the Wonders left the theater. They went to look for Hilary, who with Rachel had also been ordered to be in the theater. They had to wait until they could get her away from Pursey and Rachel, then they gathered around her in a huddle.

"You've a lot up against you," said Poppy.

"She's very finished," Alice pointed out, "and she's dancing a dance arranged by Mrs. W., so it's a showy routine."

"I'm afraid we've got to face it," Poppy added. "Your chances are bad. What I think you'd better do is to go to bed about six so you won't be tired, then go to the ballroom at six tomorrow morning so we can give you an extra hour before the proper run-through with Mr. Pinkerton at seven."

Hilary raised her chin in the air and stepped out of the huddle of Wonders.

"I won't go to bed at six, and I won't do an hour's practice before my run-through with Mr. Pinkerton. I know the routine and if the judges don't like my dance, they don't." She beamed at the Wonders. "The worst thing that can happen is that Dulcie-Pulsie has two gold watches, and though it's a sickening thought we won't die of it."

As Hilary skipped off towards her chalet Alice said:

"Hilary's clever but I doubt if she'll ever do much. I think you have to care more than she does to be a success."

But the next afternoon, watching Hilary, Alice wondered if she had been wrong. There was no doubt Hilary enjoyed the sort of dancing the Wonders learned. There was no doubt either she thought it fun imitating Dulcie. From her first entrance, mincing on conceitedly to "Girls and Boys Come Out to Play", to the amusing end where she turned cartwheels in a rather grand way before pretending to step into bed, she charmed the judges.

"Quite a card, that kiddie," said the producer of the show. "I must keep a note of her name, if she turns pro. I might use her."

The female professional dancer turned to the male professional dancer.

"Ever so neat a little dancer, didn't you think, Freddie? And unless I'm much mistaken ballet trained."

Freddie nodded.

"You couldn't be more right."

"Well," said the producer, "what marks?"

Because there were points given for originality, and all three judges gave Hilary full marks for it, her marks were nearly as high as Dulcie's had been. The producer stood up.

"Congratulations, my dear. Watch the board to see what time you dance on Saturday for the finals."

15

THE FINALS

The theater was crowded for the finals on Saturday and the judges had a horrible job. There were five of them: a professional woman singer, a man and woman who were leading amateur pair dancers, a film starlet, and a man from a television panel game.

The Wonders took Hilary to the theater early and dressed her in their dressing room.

"It's absolutely certain Dulcie won't come up here," Poppy explained, "but most of the others will. Ordinarily they use our dressing room and the chorus dressing room for these competitions, so as not to mess up the principals' rooms for the night's show. But I bet Dulcie gets put in a principal's room."

"Turn around," said Alice after she had fastened Hilary's frock; she stood away from her. "Of course we're so used to the frocks we can't think of anyone looking nice in them, but I must say you don't look bad, considering."

Hilary was enchanted with Betty's little-girl frock, for she felt like a real Wonder wearing it.

"Turn a cartwheel," said Poppy, "so we can see how you look underneath."

Under their uniforms the Wonders wore plain matching knickers, but for this special occasion something frilly had been thought right. So one of the Wonders had lent frilly lace-edged nylon knickers and a matching petticoat.

As Hilary turned a cartwheel only a froth of lace and frills showed. The Wonders watched her with professional approval.

"Couldn't be better," said Alice. "I always say

there's nothing to touch lace if you're working upside down."

There were fifteen finalists from whom the judges had to choose a winning girl, a winning boy and either a winning pair or second prizes for a boy and a girl. As well, there were to be small prizes for all the finalists. The talent varied. There was a boy conjurer, a girl who sang a comic song dressed as a boy, a boy who sang "I'll Walk Beside You" and another who sang "We'll Gather Lilacs," and several dancing pairs, as well as solo dancers. Before the contest started the camp manager explained how the judging would be arranged. For each turn the five judges would be given cards with the contestants' numbers on them. They would then give marks up to ten, as they saw fit for each performer or pair of performers.

"You see," the manager said, "that way it doesn't matter whether it's a singer, a dancer or conjurer they're marking. All the judges have to decide is how good each kiddie is at their speciality. Now, if everybody's ready we'll start."

The Wonders, sitting at the back of the theater, had their own marking system.

" 'We'll Gather Lilacs' won't be in the first three," said Alice. "His voice cracked."

"Nor will the conjurer," said Poppy. "Everybody

must have seen he had a card at the back of his hand."

Over the dancers the Wonders exchanged glances and turned down their thumbs, for none of the dancers came up to Dulcie's or Hilary's standard.

Between turns Alice stood up and studied the audience.

"Mrs. W.'s in the second row with Pursey. I can't see Rachel."

The other Wonders also stood up.

"She must be somewhere. Both she and Hilary were told to come and watch."

Betty dug Poppy in the ribs with her elbow.

"There she is, standing by the door."

Rachel had been looking for Hilary, and it had made her late. She had arrived panting, to find standing room only. She too was looking at the audience, for she was hoping to see Hilary. There would, she was afraid, be a terrible row if it was discovered Hilary had not been in the theater to watch Dulcie dance.

"Number fifty-one," called the manager.

Rachel was not interested, but the Wonders all leaned forward, for number fifty-one was Dulcie.

Dulcie, as she came onto the stage, was the perfect little professional. Her mother had taught her to acknowledge the applause which each child received as encouragement, with a little curtsey towards the

judges. Then, taking her time, she was to signal the
pianist that she was ready to start.

Dulcie looked simply charming and knew it. She
had a tight crimson bodice and a very full skirt which
came just to her knees. On her head was a dear little
hat with a red feather curling over her right ear. She
was wearing white socks and crimson dancing slippers.
As she raised her frock to dance she showed the proper
lace frills of the can-can dancer.

"You won't beat that this afternoon," said the
woman pair dancer.

"I must say she's a little duck," the singer agreed.
She turned to the starlet. "What do you think?"

The starlet was a starlet because of her figure, and
seldom thought sensibly.

"I don't know—really I don't—it's so difficult, isn't
it . . . ?"

"It's not difficult at all, my dear young lady," said
the man from the panel game, who could not endure
silly girls. "Either you think the child can dance or
you don't. It's as simple as that. Personally I loathe
the can-can."

The starlet giggled.

"I'm afraid judging isn't one of my things."

When Dulcie's dance finished there was the first
real applause of the evening.

"We must not be influenced by that," said the panel

game expert. "We must mark each child by our own standards." He looked severely at the starlet and added: "Those of us who have standards."

"I'll Walk Beside You" came next. He sang very well indeed.

"I'll take a bet that's first prize for boys," said Poppy, and she was quite right. Then she gripped hold of the Wonder next to her, for the manager had called out number forty-seven.

Mrs. Wintle was so proud of Dulcie she felt as if she had blown up like a balloon. Her ears lapped up what those around her had said. "That's the winner for sure." "Proper little professional, and ever so pretty." "As far as I can see that's the end of the contest." "I bet those five judges have given that kiddie full marks if they know what's what."

"She was good, wasn't she, Pursey?" Mrs. Wintle whispered. "Weren't you proud?"

Pursey was feeling uncomfortable. It had been all very well going with Hilary to rehearsals, but she felt very different now that she was sitting in the theater beside Mrs. Wintle. She told herself it was only a children's talent contest, and what did it matter anyway, but one glance at Mrs. Wintle out of the corner of her eye and her hopeful thoughts died. To Mrs. Wintle the result of the talent contest was enormously important, and it was outside her imagining that any children whom she taught would dance anywhere unless she said they might.

Waiting to be called, Hilary had a low mood. She wandered round the dressing room, annoying the mothers of the other children by kicking at the chairs with her awkward-Adas. Why was she doing anything so silly as going in for the contest? Rachel would be angry, Rachel's Aunt Cora would be angry, and she would not win. Nobody could beat Dulcie so why try? She almost sneaked out of the theater and went back to her chalet. But just as she was thinking how nice it would be in her chalet a woman who was helping to run the contest came to fetch her.

"Number forty-seven?" she asked, and when Hilary said that was her number she held out a hand. "Come along then, you're next."

At those words Hilary suddenly stopped feeling low, and, as had happened when she had danced in the garden at Folkestone with the tea cloths, her spirits shot into the air like a firework. Cheerfully she skipped down the stairs.

"Nervous?" asked the woman.

Hilary smiled up at her.

"Not a bit. I shall like doing my dance."

"Good, I hope it goes well."

"It's got to go well. Do you know I've worked and worked, which is something I never do, just simply to win that beautiful, beautiful gold wrist watch."

The woman laughed.

"You mercenary little thing! What about the honor and glory of winning?"

"Oh, them," said Hilary. "I can't explain, but quite truthfully if I win there wouldn't be much of that, more rage I should think. But I wouldn't care. Imagine a wrist watch! I don't know how I could bear the glory."

They were nearing the stage, where the boy was singing "I'll Walk Beside You." The woman signalled to Hilary they must be very quiet, then she stooped down and kissed her.

"Good luck. I hope you win the watch."

Feeling gay and not caring was just right for Hilary's dance. As her number was called she ran onto the stage looking as if she were twinkling all over, and because she looked so pleased the audience felt pleased, and clapped a little louder.

The panel game player looked at Hilary with approval. He liked to see little girls dressed as little girls.

The audience were charmed with Hilary, for she made them laugh, which none of the other children had done. The judges too were delighted with her, but she set them a problem. How were they to mark her amusing take-off of a dance against Dulcie's clever, well-arranged performance? The Wonders, listening to the laughter and applause, felt as if each one of them were Hilary's proud mother. But two people in the audience were not charmed, delighted or proud. They were Mrs. Wintle and Rachel.

Pursey, though she had watched Hilary rehearsing each morning, had no idea what sort of dance she was doing. To her, dancing was dancing. Some did it better than others, that was all, and she knew from what Pat and Ena had told her that Hilary was good. So it was a great puzzle to her when Mrs. Wintle was annoyed not only that Hilary was dancing without permission, but also at what she was dancing. Of course, with people sitting all round her who might know who she was, Mrs. Wintle could not be angry out loud, but in a hissing sort of whisper she let Pursey know how she felt.

"Preposterous!" "How dare the child!" "I suppose she thinks this dance funny, I think it merely silly." "I wonder whom she thinks she is amusing, certainly not me." "I wonder whom she thinks she is imitating . . ."

Rachel watched Hilary with a kind of sick fascination. It was no good trying to stop her, she could not make her voice carry above the laughter of the audience. If Madame Raine could see Hilary now, what would she say? But worse, far worse, what would her mother say if she could come back? Imagine her face! "Oh Mummie," she thought, "I'm terribly sorry. But however angry everyone is I'll do my absolute best to see it never happens again."

But it did happen again, and happened that very evening, for when the marks were added up it was found that Dulcie and Hilary had tied for the first place.

The manager came on to make the announcement.

"Two children have tied for the top place. Number fifty-one, Dulcie Wintle, aged ten, who danced the can-can number, and number forty-seven, Hilary Lennox, who danced that amusing little skit. She also is ten. I have asked the judges if they will see these two little girls dance again, and perhaps slightly revise their marks so that one is first and the other is second."

"It's nonsense," said the man pair dancer. "The little can-can has it. She's a real dancer, and I ought to know."

The panel game player was bored with being a judge, but he was not putting up with being told anything by a dancer.

"Nonsense. The little fair thing wins hands down. She has personality, and that is something I know about." He turned to the starlet. "Isn't that true, my dear?"

The starlet hoped he was talking about her.

"Thanks ever so."

Dulcie was furious at being tied for first place with Hilary. She thought it was a ridiculous result, and she was extra angry because it had happened in front of the Wonders.

"I don't think I'll bother to dance again," she told the Wonders' head matron, who was looking after her. "Let Hilary take the prize if she's so keen."

"I think I'd dance again if I were you, dear," the matron answered gently. "The people in the audience will be upset if you don't, and your mother wouldn't like that."

Sulkily Dulcie agreed. But feeling cross and sulky is not the best mood in which to dance a can-can, so it happened that though her footwork was just as good, something that had been there the first time was missing when Dulcie danced again.

Hilary, on the other hand, was overjoyed at having tied with Dulcie, and charmed to dance again.

"I've still got a chance for that watch," she told the woman who had fetched her from the dressing room. "Please hold your thumbs for me."

Because Hilary was in such wild spirits her dance

was even better the second time than it had been the first. Neither the professional dancers nor the panel game man changed their marks, nor did the starlet, but the professional singer did, giving more marks to Hilary.

The manager took Dulcie by one hand and Hilary by the other, and led them forward.

"Well, you all want to get off to your suppers, so I won't keep you. This little lady comes first," he looked at Hilary, "so this little lady is second," and he beamed at Dulcie. Then he nodded to the starlet. "So if you please, my dear, would you hand the first prize to Hilary Lennox, and the second to Dulcie Wintle, daughter I may say of the famous Mrs. Wintle, whose Wonders have been such a success here this summer. I think we can all agree little Dulcie is a chip off the old block."

Mrs. Wintle, beaming as if the result delighted her, left the theater holding Dulcie by one hand and Hilary by the other. Graciously she accepted congratulations for both.

"It's all in the family really. Yes, Hilary is my ward. Yes, Dulcie will be dancing professionally as soon as she's twelve."

Outside the theatre Rachel, blind and deaf to what was going on around her, waited for Hilary. It was dreadful what had happened. Winning a watch, which of course was something every child wanted, was the worst thing that could be imagined. No child winning a watch for awful dancing could remember words like position and line. Oh, what would her mother have said if she could have seen her?

Hilary knew she was in for a row with Rachel's Aunt Cora, but she did not care. "Oh glory, glory," her heart sang, "look at Hilary Lennox wearing a real gold watch. Who's afraid of the big bad wolf?" Then suddenly, pushing people to right and left, Rachel was in front of her. Her eyes looked enormous, and her face was pale. She spoke loud enough for all the people round to hear.

"Are you dead to decency, Hilary? You know what Madame said about high kicks and cartwheels. You know what Mummie hoped for you. If she'd seen you doing that dance she would have been sick on the floor." She clutched at Hilary's right wrist. "Give me that watch. You're not to have it. I'll give it back . . . I'll throw it in the sea . . . I'll . . ."

Whatever else Rachel planned to do with the watch the listening people never knew. For in a voice which made many of them feel slivers of ice sliding down their spines, Mrs. Wintle said:

"Pursey. Take Rachel away and put her to bed. She must be ill."

16

THE AUTUMN TERM

Although when Rachel went to sleep that night it seemed as if nothing would ever come right again, by the next morning yesterday's troubles were already blowing away like mist before a breeze.

The first person to help blow them away was Hilary. Rachel woke up to find her bouncing up and down on her bed, singing to the tune of "Three Blind Mice":

"Hilary's got a watch,
Hilary's got a watch,
Hilary's got a watch.
Oh glory be,
Oh glory be,
Oh glory be.
Who could imagine Hilary wearing a watch,
A simply glorious golden watch,
A watch that every Wonder wants,
Oh Hilary's got a watch,
Hilary's got a watch,
Hilary's got a watch."

When Hilary saw Rachel's eyes were open, in one spring she was across the chalet and sitting on the end of her bed.

"I was thinking, it'll be our watch. You'll wear it one day, and I'll wear it the next."

Rachel sat up. Her face felt, looked and sounded like a cold, because of crying the night before.

"I wouldn't wear it, it's yours."

Hilary thought that idiotic.

"We've always shared everything. If you had a gold watch you'd let me wear it."

Rachel knew that was true.

"Yes, but I won't wear yours." She hugged her knees, trying to find words to explain what she meant. "I'm truly sorry I said all that about throwing it in the sea. I didn't mean it. I meant to tell you last night only . . ."

Hilary interrupted.

"Pursey told me, but you were asleep when I came to bed."

"But I did mean you shouldn't have won it for that sort of dancing. Imagine what Madame Raine would have thought if she'd seen you."

Hilary nearly made a face to show how little she cared what Madame Raine thought. Instead she wriggled up the bed and got into it beside Rachel. She held up her wrist so that Rachel could hear her watch tick.

"She'd have thought my dancing absolutely awful, too awful to be true, I shouldn't wonder. But she is sensible, so I think she would have said: 'But if that sort of dancing was the only way you could win a gold watch, Hilary dear, then I'm glad you did it.'"

Rachel knew that Hilary knew Madame Raine would never have said anything of the sort.

"It was truly terrible dancing, especially that bit where you were upside down."

Hilary tried to look as if she was ashamed, but instead she laughed.

"Half of me is sorry you're angry, but most of me is glad about the watch. But to make up I'll promise you something on my awkward-Adas." She raised a hand. "I swear to work like a slave at ballet next term, and, though I still want the pocket money, I'll be working because of my swear and not because of the two-and-six."

The next person to help was Pursey; it was when she was doing Rachel's hair.

"Your Aunt Cora is taking Dulcie to see some friends today," she said, as if her news had nothing to do with last night's troubles. "That Mr. Pinkerton and his boys are playing at church service this morning. What were you planning to do after, my lambkin?"

"Uncle Tom said I'd find him painting on the beach."

Pursey pinned Rachel's second plait firmly in place. Then she gave her a kiss.

"You enjoy yourself, and remember that next Sunday we'll be back in London."

The last person to help clear the watch trouble away was Uncle Tom. He had seen Dulcie dressed up for her dance, but he had not taken in where and when she was dancing. He had not heard a word about a talent contest, and so of course it was not mentioned. It is very difficult to worry about anything when you are sitting on hot sand with a blue sea in front of you, cliffs behind you blazing with poppies, and between you and your uncle there is a basket with a gorgeous luncheon inside it. Rachel did think for a moment of telling Uncle Tom the whole story, but she knew that though he would listen, he would not think it very important. At that moment Rachel almost wondered herself if it were important.

All the next week Rachel expected a summons to talk to Aunt Cora, but it never came. She supposed this was because Aunt Cora thought sending her to bed was punishment enough. But she had not heard a conversation between Pursey and Mrs. Wintle on Monday morning.

"I've been thinking, Pursey," Mrs. Wintle said, "that I'll send Rachel to a boarding school. She'll never make a dancer, and I don't think I can stand much more of her."

They had met in the theater, where Pursey was having a final check of the Wonders' apple blossom dresses. She spoke quietly.

"The day you send Rachel away, I give up the school."

Mrs. Wintle turned a sort of plum color from

shock, for she looked upon Pursey as a dear kind old
sheep, who never said things like that.

"What do you mean, Pursey?"

"What I say. Of course Rachel's behaved badly
about the dancing, but she knows it, so there's no
need to say any more. You know, Mrs. W., at last
Rachel's settling in with us, and in time she'll get
into our ways. Sending her away now, where she
couldn't keep an eye on Hilary, would be downright
wicked."

Mrs. Wintle was so angry her words came out on
top of each other.

"What impertinence . . . whose niece is she . . . I
won't be interfered with. . . ."

Pursey picked one of the apple blossom dresses off
its peg and looked it over.

"Do what you like, Mrs. W., but if Rachel leaves
the school I go too, and that's my last word. And if
you'll take some advice I would forget Saturday. After
all, you can't put milk that has been upset back in the
bottle, so what I say is let it lie."

Of course just not saying anything did not make
Rachel easier with Aunt Cora, or Aunt Cora fonder of
Rachel. But luckily for Rachel the autumn term was
that year busier than usual, and Mrs. Wintle had no
time to waste on such an unimportant person as

Rachel. So Rachel was able to get through the whole term without one row with her aunt.

Hilary, stimulated by her holiday with the Wonders, was for her really working at her dancing. This meant that she not only kept her promise to Rachel but, which Rachel did not know, worked so hard at her tap, acrobatics and musical comedy that her progress was considered by Pat and Ena to be startling.

"Hilary, if she keeps it up, will be a better dancer than Dulcie," Ena whispered to Pat.

"I know, Pat," Ena whispered back, "but don't be too hopeful. Dulcie is ambitious and Hilary is not."

Rachel had more than Pat's word about Hilary's ballet work, for one day she watched her. It was Pat's idea.

"I keep telling you Hilary's working, but if you really want to know how she's getting on come and see for yourself."

A few days later Rachel, having asked Mrs. Storm's permission, slipped quietly into the classroom where Pat was giving Hilary her lesson.

Rachel watched Hilary's lesson with the pride of a mother. My goodness, she thought, real Royal Ballet School dancing. Even Madame Raine would be pleased. If Hilary could be made to go on working like this for four more years everything would come right. Somehow she, Rachel, would find a way to earn

enough money for Hilary to go to The Royal Ballet
School. Pursey had said she need not be a Wonder
after she was fifteen. Very quietly, so as not to disturb
Hilary, she crept out of the room.

"Oh glory," she thought as she ran back to the
schoolroom, "in spite of everything Hilary's learning
to be a real proper dancer like Mummie wanted. Oh,
glory, glory!"

As Pat had hoped, Rachel was moved up into
Group three that term. In Group three she found herself working with girls of her own age. They were, of
course, dud Wonders, but that suited her, for she was
able more or less to keep up with them. As well, after
a day or two, she began to like them and make friends
with some of them. Rachel would never be as popular
as Hilary was, for she was a much quieter sort of person. Also, which the Wonders thought odd, she did
not think being a good Wonder was important. When
Pat or Ena praised the others they were thrilled, but
Rachel did not care whether she was praised or not.

To the Wonders another odd thing about Rachel
was that she took no interest in auditions. In the first
half of the term parties of Wonders went to auditions
almost every Saturday, shepherded by Pat or Ena, or,
when it was Group one, by Mrs. Wintle herself.

It was Mrs. Wintle's ambition that every child old
enough to be licensed should be engaged at Christmas,

and that year it looked as though she would achieve her ambition. The twenty-four Blackpool Wonders were only just back at the school when the whole lot were engaged to go to Newcastle for *Mother Goose*.

The holiday camp Wonders were after four auditions engaged for a pantomime in outer London.

"It's wonderful to be back in old London," said Poppy. "It was gorgeous in the camp, but enough's enough."

"When your holidays start," Alice whispered to Hilary, "I'll see if I can talk matron into letting you come and watch one of our rehearsals."

The *Look up and Smile* troupe was broken up.

"They're too plain, that lot," said Mrs. Wintle, "to be kept together. We'll mix them up with the rest of Group one, and see if that way we can get them all into first-class panto."

The *Look up and Smile Wonders* knew what was happening to them.

"I wish she wouldn't separate us," Anne said sadly to Hilary. "You can think how humiliated you feel when you are sent out with the good lookers, and you have to hear, as I've done six times, 'Little fat girl, fourth from the left, will you stand out.' Then back I come without an engagement."

But in the end all the *Look up and Smile* Wonders were placed, most of them, as Mrs. Wintle had hoped, in the grandest Christmas shows. By the end of auditions even most of those licensed in Group three were placed.

Rachel watched the Wonders marching off to auditions with a cold feeling in her inside. As girls who were not much better dancers than she was came back with engagements she felt as if she were in a lift that was coming down too fast. How would she bear it when she had to wear a little-girl frock and carry a case with her shoes in it, and go to an audition? How terrible if, when she went to an audition, a manager engaged her as a Wonder. Each night when she said her prayers she added:

"Oh God, if I have to be a Wonder, would you help me to get used to the idea before I'm twelve."

17

FESTIVALS

Dulcie's birthday in November had been so big an
occasion that Hilary had great hopes about Rachel's
and her own birthdays. Dulcie's birthday was the day
on which Mrs. Wintle gave all the Wonders an early
Christmas party. There were presents for everybody,
a grand tea with an enormous birthday cake cut by
Dulcie, and what Mrs. Wintle called the birthday

throne and crown. The throne was an ordinary chair made to look splendid by an arch of leaves and flowers. The crown, which Dulcie wore all through the party, was the sort a fairy queen would wear.

"She didn't say it was only Dulcie's crown," Hilary said hopefully to Rachel after the party was over. "You're a niece and I'm almost one. Wouldn't it be terrific if we had parties like that on our birthdays and wore that stupendous crown? I'd feel too grand to be true."

"I'd hate it," Rachel said. "If I have a birthday party what I'd like would be to go to a theater."

Hilary's eyes twinkled.

"Don't say it, I've guessed. We'd all go to Covent Garden."

"I'd like that," Rachel agreed, "but what I'd like better would be a play of Shakespeare's, especially *Henry the Fifth,* where that boy comes I learned in the summer holidays."

Hilary fell flat on the floor pretending to faint.

"Oh my goodness! You wouldn't want that, not on a birthday. You couldn't, Rachel."

"I shouldn't worry, it won't happen. I can't see Aunt Cora asking me what I would like to do, can you?"

"No," Hilary agreed, "she never would."

Christmas Day was as nice a day for Rachel and

Hilary as Pursey, Uncle Tom, Wanda and Yolanta could make it. By what Hilary said could only be described as "gorgeous luck," two days before Christmas Mrs. Wintle had to rush up to Newcastle. Mumps had broken out in what had in the summer been the Blackpool troupe, and three Wonders had caught it. An ill Wonder ceased to be a Wonder to Mrs. Wintle, and became just a tiresome child.

"So stupid, I suppose they have been shopping in crowded places and picked up a germ. Well, there's nothing for it but to scrape the bottom of the barrel."

The bottom of the barrel was Wonders from Group three who had not been engaged even as understudies. Now the best of them would have to join the troupe.

Mrs. Wintle decided that as Dulcie had already had mumps she could go with her.

"I'll take you with me, darling. You can help me teach those stupid children the routines. It'll be hard work but we can't let the name of Wintle be disgraced, can we?"

Rachel and Hilary saw the departure of Mrs. Wintle, Dulcie and the three Wonders from their bedroom window.

"Poor, poor beasts," said Hilary, as she saw the last blue duffle coat vanish into a taxi. "I should think it'll be a Christmas they'll never forget. Traveling with Aunt Cora and Dulcie-Pulsie, knowing inside them that however hard they work they'll never get the routines right because it isn't in them. It's cruel!"

Rachel turned away from the window.

"Thank goodness it isn't me. But it will be when I'm twelve, for my natural niche as a Wonder will be the bottom of the barrel."

Hilary giggled. Then, propped against the end of her bed, she stood on her hands.

"Anyway, they've gone. Oh glorious day! Never, never did I think anything so perfect could happen as both Aunt Cora and Dulcie being away for Christmas."

In Newcastle something exciting for Dulcie happened. The manager of the theatre saw Dulcie trying to teach the new girls a dance routine. He watched her for some time, then found Mrs. Wintle.

"Has your Dulcie just had her eleventh birthday?"

Mrs. Wintle nodded.

"That's a brilliant kiddie you've got, Mrs. W. What's her singing like?"

"She has quite a nice voice."

"Got an audition routine?"

"I could arrange one. Why?"

"I think she's a star in the making, and I'd like to give her a chance. If she can speak lines and sing I could use her next Christmas, for I'm doing *Red Riding Hood* as my London Panto."

Two days later a contract was signed for Dulcie to star in *Red Riding Hood* the following Christmas. The result of this was that Dulcie came back from Newcastle terribly conceited. Rachel could escape quite often to Uncle Tom's studio, and there forget Dulcie and everything else through the pages of a book. But Hilary had a great deal to suffer. She would slip, as she hoped unnoticed, into a practice room and would be happily working at acrobatics when the door would open and Dulcie come in. Dulcie would watch Hilary for a minute or two with an amused smile, then say condescendingly:

"You're doing that wrong. Let me show you."

The miserable thing was that Dulcie could show how dancing and acrobatics should be done. But there are ways and ways of showing, and Dulcie's was the worst way. Hilary did not endure in silence.

"I don't want to be shown. Ena will show me in class. I'd rather do it wrong than have you show me anything."

Dulcie looked smug.

"I shall tell Mum you're being silly, and that you wouldn't let me help you. Considering I've been engaged to play *Red Riding Hood* it's pretty nice of me to bother with you."

"I don't want you to bother," Hilary would retort. "I want you to go away."

Then Dulcie would walk on her hands, or do a flip-flap, or turn a cartwheel, all of which she did beautifully. When she was the right way up again she would say:

"You see. That's how it ought to look." Then, before Hilary had time to answer, she would skip out of the room.

Two or three times a week Mrs. Wintle took all three children and Pursey to the theater. It was a repetition of the summer holiday; at each theater Wonders were appearing, so at each theater out came Mrs. Wintle's notebook. Dulcie's criticisms, now that she was engaged for *Red Riding Hood,* came more often than they had in the summer, and she was even grander during the visit to the dressing rooms. Pursey, who knew how Rachel and Hilary felt, would find an opportunity to soothe them.

"Don't let her upset you, she doesn't upset the Wonders."

"But she's so despising," Hilary would complain.

"I daresay, dear," Pursey would agree, "but it's no wonder. Booked to star a year before she can have a license, which never happened to any other Wonder, was bound to go to her head. But you watch, pride will come before a fall."

Because everyone was busy Hilary was afraid Rachel's birthday would be forgotten, so she went round reminding the household about it. She started with Pursey.

"Pursey, it's Rachel's birthday next week."

Pursey looked up from the shopping list she was making.

"I'm glad you reminded me, I must tell Wanda to make her a cake, and we'll want eleven candles."

"Will she have her chair decorated, and wear a crown like Dulcie did?"

Pursey looked flustered.

"Oh no, dear, that's special for Dulcie." Then her face cleared. "Anyway Rachel wouldn't want it."

"Then what will happen for Rachel? She always had a gorgeous birthday at Folkestone."

Pursey, her mind half on the Wonders' wardrobes and half on Rachel's birthday, could not make a decision.

"I don't know, dear. Why don't you speak to her Uncle? He's the one for plans."

It was difficult for Hilary to see Uncle Tom alone, for so often Rachel was in the studio, but the next morning she caught him while Rachel was working at her tap. She was so afraid Rachel would finish her practice before she had time to talk to Uncle Tom that she burst into the studio talking as she came.

"It's Rachel's birthday on Wednesday, she can't have a crown and special chair because they belong to

Dulcie, and except for a cake Wanda's making and a chocolate fish and a piece of soap made like a dog I've bought her, nothing's happening at all, and . . ."

Uncle Tom stopped painting and looked with a laugh on his face at Hilary.

"That's not all. I've bought Rachel a present I know she'll like."

"What?"

"I shan't tell you, wait and see. But I hadn't thought about how the day was to be spent. What would Rachel like to do?"

Hilary had a fight with herself before she could make herself tell the truth.

"To see one of Shakespeare's beastly plays. Can you imagine? How could a child think seeing Shakespeare a birthday thing?"

Uncle Tom laughed.

"Plenty do." He fetched a paper which was on a table and turned up the theater list. "I'm not sure what the Old Vic is doing. I think it'll be *Twelfth Night*. How would she like that?"

"She wanted *Henry the Fifth,* but I think *Twelfth Night* will do splendidly."

"Good. I'll book us seats."

"Us? You hadn't thought I'd want to go, had you?"

Uncle Tom ruffled Hilary's hair.

"You are a card! I hadn't thought you'd want to go

but you're going, for that sister of yours won't enjoy her birthday party unless you're there. And I shall try and get Dulcie to come too. It's time she saw some good plays."

Hilary looked at him as if he were a stupid child.

"Dulcie will hate it, and, quite truthfully, though I know Dulcie is your child, I must point out Rachel won't really enjoy having her."

Uncle Tom gave Hilary an affectionate pat on her behind.

"Run along, and leave the arranging to me. If Rachel and Dulcie don't get on it's high time they did."

Although she hated doing it, Hilary also reminded Aunt Cora about Rachel's birthday. She saw her having luncheon with Dulcie and, though she was scared, she marched up to their table.

Aunt Cora looked up with a why-interrupt-me-now look on her face.

"What is it?"

"I thought perhaps you'd forgotten it's Rachel's birthday next Wednesday."

Aunt Cora had forgotten, but she was not going to admit it.

"Yes . . . yes, I know it is."

Dulcie was not going to be left out.

"You needn't bother. We're giving her a present, aren't we, Mum?"

Aunt Cora, though she was generous, had no time for shopping, so what she did was to tell Pursey to buy something that Rachel would like, and to order a box of chocolates for Dulcie to give.

Rachel enjoyed her birthday. Not knowing that Pursey had chosen them she was amazed to get book ends from Aunt Cora. But what thrilled her was Uncle Tom's present. For when she opened his parcel she found inside a gold wrist watch.

"Imagine," she said to Hilary, "we've both got one now."

Hilary was as pleased as Rachel was.

"And come as a birthday present, not dancing as a Wonder, so you needn't be ashamed of it."

Dulcie refused to go to the theater party.

"No thank you, Dad, I'll go again to *Aladdin* with Mum. There's a good dancer in it Mum wants me to watch."

To make up to Hilary for having to sit through *Twelfth Night* Uncle Tom bought a large box of chocolates which Hilary almost finished during the first half of the play. The result of this was that she slept through the second half.

"It was either going to sleep or being sick," she told Rachel as they undressed for bed. "I felt most peculiar, but luckily it wore off by the time I woke up."

Rachel was standing by the window.

" 'If music be the food of love, play on'. . . . what heavenly words. Because I've seen *Twelfth Night,* almost I don't mind being eleven though it means only a year left before I'm a Wonder."

18

BEING ELEVEN

Being eleven meant a great deal in Mrs. Wintle's
school. When you were eleven you worked both for
a solo and a troupe audition and had special singing
lessons. When you were eleven you became more important because you would soon stop being a training
Wonder and become a working Wonder.

Because they were so busy the year skimmed by. Hilary moved up into Group one, and she had her birthday. To her disgust there was no crown or throne, but there was a large cake and a special tea for her group, and Mrs. Storm took her, Dulcie and Rachel to Madame Tussaud's. Easter came round again, and there was a picnic on Good Friday with Pursey, and an egg-hunt on Easter Day. Then it was summer again, and once more they were all visiting the Wonders. Then, before it seemed possible, it was autumn and all Wonders old enough for a license were marched to auditions. But this year there was a difference.

"We don't want the same trouble we had last year," said Mrs. Wintle to Pat and Ena. "So I want stand-ins who know the routines trained in advance, so they can be sent off at once if there is illness."

"What about Rachel, Mrs. W.?" Pat asked. "She will be twelve in January."

"Train her," said Mrs. Wintle. "It would indeed be scraping the barrel if I were forced to use her, but there is no harm in having her ready in case."

Rachel heard the news that she was to be trained as a stand-by Wonder in resigned silence. That evening when she was undressing for bed she told Hilary what was to happen.

"It means I'll be taken to the County Hall for a license on my birthday, I should think. I wish the London County Council wouldn't give me a license."

"They will," said Hilary. "You're terribly good at lessons, and you're not ill. Those are the things they care about."

"I know," Rachel agreed, "and I've accepted my fate. Ever since I got here I've asked in my prayers that when I'm twelve I won't mind being a Wonder. They say everybody gets the strength they need for the cross they have to bear. I can feel I'm getting strength to bear being a Wonder, even if it means being an elf like the Aladdin Wonders were last Christmas."

Hilary giggled at the memory of the Aladdin Wonders.

"Pixies they were, not elves, peeping out of tree trunks. I must say they were awful."

Mrs. Storm was Rachel's other confidante.

"I've got to stand by for the Group three Wonders when I'm twelve, in January."

Mrs. Storm was not surprised.

"I guessed you would soon be working. I'm sorry. I'm afraid you'll hate it."

"It'll be beastly," Rachel agreed, "but you can be resigned to anything."

"That's true," said Mrs. Storm, "and I've helped prepare you for the evil day."

Rachel was surprised.

"How?" she wanted to know.

"All the parts I've taught you. Even the hardest working troupe of Wonders gets time between entrances. You've got plenty of parts you can work at in your head while you're not on the stage."

Rachel looked doubtful.

"I don't think the Wonders are supposed to sit and think. I've heard Aunt Cora say lots of times 'Are you having fun, kiddiewinks?'. And by fun she means playing games in the dressing room with the matrons."

"What sort of games?"

"All sorts, such as who can think of most things beginning with A, and card games."

"But I don't suppose you have to play games if you don't want to."

"I don't know, never having been a Wonder, but from what I've heard all Wonders play games. It's considered unsporting not to."

"I see," said Mrs. Storm, who did not see at all. "Now let me hear that speech of Viola's."

Being a stand-by meant very hard work for Rachel. For there were three troupes of Wonders with engagements near London in Group three; twelve in *Mother Goose,* twelve working in a small show called *Christmas Belles,* and eight were to be toys in a children's play.

"I'll never learn it all," Rachel told Hilary. "It isn't that it's difficult, but it's all different. If any Wonder gets ill I should think I'd be certain to do the wrong dance in the wrong show."

"You won't," said Hilary. "The clothes will help. You couldn't dance as a gosling from *Mother Goose* when you're dressed as a toy soldier, as you would be if it was *Christmas Belles*."

All through the autumn term Dulcie worked at her part in *Red Riding Hood*. She was sent to a voice production teacher for her lines, but she had as well to work at them with Mrs. Storm. Hilary found Dulcie being Little Red Riding Hood excruciatingly funny, and she would make Rachel laugh imitating her. It was all exaggerated of course, and not in the least fair to Dulcie, who, as Hilary admitted, was likely to be a great success.

"And of course her dancing really is good," she would say, "and though I don't like the way she does it I must own she puts over a number awfully well."

Mrs. Storm watched the preparations for Dulcie's first appearance with apparent tolerance, but at home she said to her husband:

"If that child is a success she will be intolerable next term."

Her husband knew all about Mrs. Wintle's schoolroom.

171

"Don't worry. Fix your mind on Rachel."

Mrs. Storm was increasingly fixing her mind on Rachel. That term, as a change from Shakespeare, Mrs. Storm was teaching her a speech of Joan's from Bernard Shaw's *Saint Joan*. It was made by Joan when she learned she was not to be set free but imprisoned.

"It's difficult," Mrs. Storm explained, "but, as after Christmas you may be working as a Wonder where you will only learn the latest songs, I think for our lessons we should try difficult things."

Rachel, Mrs. Storm found, was good as Joan. It seemed as if in a way she understood her. For when she pleaded not to be shut away from the sun, or from the bells which were her voices, she was a real person.

"I liked that," Mrs. Storm said one day, "and as a reward I shall ask if I may take you to a theater this Christmas. Not Shakespeare this time, but a modern play. Would you like that?"

Rachel's eyes shone.

"Oh thank you, it will be something to look forward to, which I shall need this Christmas with my twelfth birthday hanging over me."

19

RED RIDING HOOD

Everybody, including Wanda and Yolanta, went to Dulcie's first night. It happened two days before Christmas.

"And I'll be glad when it's over," Hilary told Rachel, "for to hear the fuss you'd think *Red Riding Hood* was more important than Christmas Day."

As well as Dulcie there were twelve Wonders in the pantomime, carefully picked to make Dulcie look even smaller and more dainty than she was. So, as Pursey said in her cozy voice as she read the programme:

"Nobody can miss the name Wintle, that's a certainty."

Although Rachel did not care for pantomimes, nobody can help feeling a thrill as the house lights dim and the curtain rises. The first scene in *Red Riding Hood* was a village street. The chorus came on, dancing to and singing a song which began "Hurrah, Hurray. We've got a holiday." Then from both sides of the stage, wearing print frocks and sunbonnets, or shorts, shirts and little straw hats, on bounced the twelve Wonders. Then came two funny men, and then it was Dulcie's entrance.

Dulcie wore a short frilly frock, white socks, red awkward-Adas and a little cape and hood of red taffeta. She looked delightful. Soon after her first entrance, she sang a song. It was about a doll, and behind her the Wonders danced dressed as dolls.

There was no doubt about it, the audience loved Dulcie. As she sang and danced a sort of coo rose from the theater. "Isn't she a love?" "What a beautiful little dancer." "Isn't she clever?" "Can't be more than eight."

Nobody clapped louder than Hilary.

"Whatever I feel about her I have to admit she's awfully good," she whispered to Rachel.

Even Rachel was carried away.

"Isn't she? But for goodness sake don't want to be like her."

As the pantomime went on Aunt Cora felt prouder and prouder. In fact the only blot, on what was the most perfect evening she had ever spent, was when one of the Wonders fell over when she should have been walking on her hands. Out came the famous notebook. Pursey made tch-tch-ing sounds.

"Poor Agnes, ever so nice a girl. Must be slippery on the stage."

"Nonsense," said Mrs. Wintle, writing hard. "Stick to your wardrobe, Pursey, you know nothing about acrobatics. Agnes fell because she timed her throw forward badly."

"I'm surprised all twelve haven't fallen over," Hilary whispered to Rachel. "It must be the worst thing that could happen to be a Wonder in the show in which Dulcie is a star. Imagine!"

At the end of the pantomime, when all the artistes marched down a grand staircase, the audience had a chance to show Dulcie how much they had enjoyed her performance. She came down alone, wearing a white net frock trimmed with silver stars. She still

175

had on her crimson cape, but round her head was a wreath of silver flowers and on her feet silver slippers. As she ran down the steps and curtsied to the audience there was a roar from the theater.

"I think we can say," Aunt Cora whispered to Uncle Tom, "our child is a smash hit."

After the performance there was the usual visit backstage, but of course this time the first call was to Dulcie's dressing room. She had a room to herself, with a matron to look after and dress her. When her family arrived she had just changed from her last-act frock and was wearing a dressing gown while she took off her make-up. Rachel and Hilary's first impression was that success had made Dulcie nicer. She was very excited, but then who would not be, but she was not a bit stand-offish or grand. To their great surprise she hugged first Rachel and then Hilary, and asked them if she had been good. Then, when they said she was marvelous, she pointed to an enormous box of chocolates the management had sent her and told them to help themselves.

"Too un-Dulcie-ish to last," whispered Hilary to Rachel, picking out a chocolate with a crystallized violet on the top. "Almost I like her."

The visit to the Wonders was just like all grand tours of a Wonders' dressing room. But this time there was something for the Wonders to say.

"Wasn't Dulcie good, Mrs. Wintle?" they chorused.

"You must be feeling proud, Mrs. W.," said the matron.

Mrs. Wintle smiled.

"Thank you, kiddiewinks, thank you, matron, but we mustn't let Dulcie's success blind us to our faults, must we?" She opened her notebook. "I shall want you all at the school tomorrow to tidy up some bad work. As for you, Agnes . . ."

Hilary was right, the niceness of Dulcie after her first night did not last. It was not altogether Dulcie's fault, for although Pursey and Uncle Tom tried to make her remember that one success does not make a star, Aunt Cora talked to her very stupidly, calling her "Mum's little leading lady." Also, Dulcie's life in the theater made her have too good an opinion of herself. Her mother had spent too long in the theater to allow a child of hers to behave badly in front of the principals or the management. But in the dressing room she was a very different child.

At first Rachel and Hilary's news of Dulcie in the dressing room was hearsay from Betty, that same Betty who had lent her little-girl frock to Hilary for the talent contest. Betty was Dulcie's understudy, and before the pantomime opened she had been very pleased about her engagement.

But soon after the pantomime started Betty became gloomy.

"I'm being made to sit in Dulcie's room. It's terrible."

"What's she want you there for?" Hilary asked.

"Just as a slave," said Betty. "One matron isn't enough, she has to have me too. Betty, pick that up. Betty, hold this. Betty, run up to the Wonders' dressing room and fetch me some milk. I'm like one of those slaves the Romans had who had to row a ship chained to the seat."

The next news came a few days later. Hilary was practicing acrobatics when Betty burst into the room.

"Have you seen any of the Red Riding Hood Wonders?" Hilary shook her head. "Well, you ought to hear them. They're mad as wasps."

Hilary, who had been trying to walk on her hands, turned the right way up.

"What's happened?"

Betty had come for a tap lesson. She limbered up before she answered.

"You know how we play games and have tea between shows. Well it's been great fun, and we've got a new game with cars that you guide with a magnet. Now Dulcie comes to tea with us, and we only play the games she chooses."

Hilary was amazed.

"Why should she go into the Wonders' dressing room when she's got a posh one of her own?"

Betty practiced a few steps.

"She gets bored. Luckily she has to have half an hour's rest on her sofa, so we're spared that. But then up she comes, so grand you'd think we all ought to curtsey. 'Hullo, matron. Hullo, girls,' she says, then she sits in a chair as if it was her birthday throne, and picks on one of us and says: 'Bring me my tea.' "

Before Hilary could hear more Ena fetched Betty for her lesson. But two days later she and Rachel found out for themselves what was going on. They were having breakfast with Pursey when Aunt Cora came in.

"Good morning, dears. I've got a treat for you today. I'm sending you to the theater with Dulcie."

Hilary looked as if she might be going to say something which Aunt Cora would not like, so Pursey spoke first.

"I might go with them. I want to look over the Red Riding Hood Wonders' costumes for their speciality."

"A good idea," Aunt Cora agreed. "You can bring these two home with you when the curtain goes up on the second performance."

"Can we watch from the side of the stage?" Hilary asked.

Aunt Cora nodded.

"I hope that may be allowed, but we must see what the stage manager says. I am sending him a note." She looked at Rachel. "I have planned today so that you may get some idea of stage work from the back of the theater. You must remember that by this time next week, if we should have illness, you may be working."

Rachel's inside felt as if it was turning over.

"Even if you were so pushed for Wonders that you had to use me I would hardly have got my license by this time next week, would I?"

"Don't quibble," said Aunt Cora severely. "I do hope I am soon to see some enthusiasm from you, Rachel. You are a very lucky child, you know. Few girls with as little talent as you have would have a chance to be a Wonder."

Rachel knew that Aunt Cora was right. Plenty of children would like to be Wonders. What a pity she was not one of them! But whatever happened she must not let Aunt Cora know how she felt, for if she thought she was not trying she might punish her by not letting her become something else when she was fifteen. She struggled to make her face look interested.

"I suppose I'd better watch the Wonders, for I'll never be Red Riding Hood or anybody like that, will I?"

Aunt Cora gave a short barkish sort of laugh.

"Hardly. But watching Dulcie can do you nothing

but good. She has said you and Hilary may sit in her dressing room, and if permission is granted you will go with her down to the stage, so that you can study her work closely."

"Won't that be splendid for us," said Hilary.

Aunt Cora looked at Hilary thoughtfully. Was that meant or was she being cheeky? Pursey saw what Aunt Cora was wondering. She said quickly:

"Ever so nice it will be for them, Mrs. W."

"It will," Aunt Cora agreed, "and do for goodness sake smile, Rachel. It is so disheartening when I work and plan for you to get nothing but a blank, bored expression."

Rachel had so hoped she was looking as a would-be Wonder ought to look that a lump came into her throat. She bent over her plate so that it would not show that there were nearly tears in her eyes. As it happened Aunt Cora would not have noticed, for she said no more, but went grandly out of the canteen.

Hilary managed to keep quiet until the door was shut. Then she said in an angry hiss:

"Why do you let her talk in that despising way, Rachel? Why don't you tell her you'd loathe to be a Wonder?"

Pursey patted Rachel's hand, and her voice was even cozier than usual.

"Because Rachel knows what's right, don't you, my

lambkin? All the others work when they're twelve, and you don't want to be the only one that's different, do you, dear?"

"But she doesn't want to be a Wonder, and I can't see why she doesn't say so," Hilary argued. "There must be something else she could do."

"Not at twelve there isn't," said Pursey. "When she's older it will be different."

Rachel looked up.

"When I'm fifteen. That's what you said, wasn't it, Pursey?"

Pursey hoped she had not been too optimistic, but now was not the moment to say so.

"That's right, my lamb. Time you're fifteen or so everything will be all right."

20

CHICKEN POX

Dulcie drove to and from the theater in a hired car, so that day Pursey, Rachel and Hilary drove with her.

Seeing Dulcie leave for the theater was quite an experience. Her mother had decided that Dulcie should wear a glorified version of the Wonders' outdoor uniform. This meant a very smartly tailored coat of the same blue as the Wonders' duffle coats. On her head Dulcie wore the same beret as the Wonders, but her W.W., instead of being embroidered, was on a diamond brooch. But what amazed Rachel and Hilary most was not Dulcie's clothes or her smart car, but the fact that she carried a large teddy bear. Never since they had lived with her had either Rachel or Hilary seen her cuddling anything.

"Are you going to take that bear to the theater?" Hilary asked.

Dulcie hugged her bear tighter and smiled up at the chauffeur, who was holding the car door open for her.

"'Course I'm taking Teddy. He always comes, doesn't he, Jenkins?"

Jenkins gave Dulcie what Rachel and Hilary thought a silly sort of smile.

"I reckon there wouldn't be a pantomime unless Teddy was in the theater."

Hilary's face had the screwed-up look faces get just before they laugh, so Pursey said:

"You sit in front with Mr. Jenkins, dear."

At the theater the stage doorkeeper, otherwise probably a sensible man, turned just as silly as Jenkins at the sight of Dulcie.

"How are little Miss Wintle and Mr. Teddy today?"

Dulcie put on what was known in the school as her Dulcie-Pulsie face.

184

"We're both very well, thank you. Has my mail gone up?"

The doorkeeper nodded.

"Too much for your little hands to carry. Lots of letters, some autograph albums, and two parcels which look like chocolates."

All the way to Dulcie's dressing room the same sort of talk went on. "How's Teddy?" seemed to be the sort of greeting Dulcie got from everybody. Hilary would have laughed out loud but Rachel prevented her.

"Don't. She'll only be angry, and we don't want that if we've got to sit in her dressing room."

"I'll try not to," Hilary whispered back, "but much more of this Mr. Teddy talk and I'll have to laugh or I'll blow up."

Hilary did not have to laugh or blow up, for in the dressing room with the door shut Dulcie stopped being a little girl hugging a teddy bear, and became Miss Dulcie Wintle, the star of *Red Riding Hood*.

"Good afternoon," she said to the matron, who was helping her off with her coat. "You can open my letters, Rachel, and read them to me while I'm making up. You can undo the parcels, Hilary. And Betty, as my cousins are here, I shan't want you in my room today. You can go and sit with the Wonders."

Betty, delighted, skipped out of the room. But before she left she caught Hilary's eye and, to remind her of what she had said about being a galley slave, made a rowing movement.

Pursey also went up to the Wonders' dressing room, but before she left she said to the matron:

"You're looking tired, Mrs. Mann dear."

Mrs. Mann would have liked to say she would rather have charge of sixty Wonders than one Dulcie, but she did not, for she did not want to lose her job. Instead she said:

"Well, you know how it is when it's twice daily. And Dulcie does have a lot of changes."

Pursey guessed it was Dulcie rather than hard work which was making Mrs. Mann look so tired. She was a very good matron, and Pursey did not want to lose her, so she turned to Rachel for help.

"As you're here today, you and Hilary will do everything you can to help Mrs. Mann, won't you?"

Rachel was going to say that of course they would, but Hilary spoke first.

"We'll love helping, won't we, Rachel?"

"That's very kind of you," said Mrs. Mann solemnly, but her eyes were twinkling with laughter.

The stage manager, having read Mrs. Wintle's note, gave permission, while Dulcie was on, for Rachel and Hilary to stand with Mrs. Mann on the side of the stage. In spite of finding Dulcie grand and tiresome in the dressing room, Hilary enjoyed watching her. But she enjoyed watching the Wonders even more. She was not allowed to speak to them while they were waiting for their entrances, but by signs she let them see what she thought of sitting in Dulcie's dressing room, and that she and Rachel would be up to tea later.

Rachel had her eyes glued to Dulcie, but her thoughts were miles away. She remembered the day Mrs. Storm had taken her to see a thriller and had brought her back to her house to tea afterwards, where she had met Mr. Storm. She had been allowed to roast chestnuts on the fire, which had made her feel almost as if she were back in Folkestone. It was strange to be in a proper house again, where you could do things for yourself. It was all right at the school, but there was of course no place to do things like roasting chestnuts or making toast.

But life behind the scenes with Dulcie left very little time for daydreaming. Even if she had to go on again in the same dress she needed looking after on the side of the stage. Matron had a comb, a brush, a looking glass, a powder puff, and a wrap in case there was a draught. As she had two extra helpers Dulcie used them.

"Hilary, hold this looking glass," she whispered, "so I can see if I need any powder. Give Rachel my brush, Mrs. Mann, so your hands are free to comb my hair."

It did not help either Rachel or Hilary, while being ordered about by Dulcie, that all twelve Wonders watched them with laughter that only the most strenuous efforts held inside them.

When Dulcie had to change her clothes Rachel and Hilary had to go back to the dressing room with her. There they had to obey another stream of orders.

"I wear my tap awkward-Adas for this number, Hilary. They're in the corner." "Take off these shoes, Rachel, and help Hilary put on my others."

Dulcie's changes were easy, for she wore the same frilly underclothes under all her frocks. But somehow she managed to keep Mrs. Mann and Rachel and Hilary in a continual rush, so that when it was time for her next entrance, even Hilary felt flustered.

At the end of the second act of the pantomime every character appeared in the land of flowers. This was ruled over by the Fairy Queen. The previous scene had shown Red Riding Hood being rescued from the wolf in the nick of time by the Fairy Queen. Then all the scenery changed. The wood became the land of flowers, with Dulcie as the Queen's guest, seated on a throne to watch the ballet. This meant that Dulcie was on the stage for a long time, so Mrs. Mann, Rachel and Hilary could relax.

Hilary of course watched the dancers, especially the Wonders, with absorbed interest. Mrs. Mann moved quietly upstage to have a whispered gossip with the Wonders' matron. Rachel, her eyes on the stage, was just about to slide off into another daydream when the Fairy Queen began to dance to Tschaikovsky's Sugar-Plum Fairy music. Suddenly Rachel found that she was watching, really watching, only it was not the girl who played the Fairy Queen she was looking at, but at Hilary grown taller, older, after a year or two at The Royal Ballet School. So sure was Rachel that it was Hilary she was watching that as the Fairy Queen came off-stage amidst roars of applause, she smiled at her, thinking she was smiling at Hilary.

The principal girl had a song to sing about tulip time while the chorus and the Wonders danced around her, so the Fairy Queen had a few minutes' rest. She put an arm around Rachel.

"Are you little Dulcie's cousin?" she asked in a whisper. Rachel nodded. "You aren't a bit like her. You have a dancer's face. Can you dance?"

Rachel pointed to Hilary.

"No. She can."

The Fairy Queen looked at Hilary.

"She's a good build for it. Is Mrs. Wintle training her?"

Rachel's whisper was more fierce than she knew.

"Now she is. She means to make a Wonder of her. But I won't have it. She's to go to The Royal Ballet School, and be a proper dancer like you."

"Like me!" The Fairy Queen looked half sad, half amused. "I'm afraid that won't do her much good," she whispered. "I was there; Sadler's Wells it was called then. Everybody thought I had talent, but I hadn't enough. After a time I knew it. I didn't want to be a might-have-been, so I left to be a Fairy Queen and to dance in musical comedies."

Rachel was horrified.

"Don't tell Hilary about you. At the moment she wants to be a Wonder and it's only me who means her to go to The Royal Ballet School."

The Fairy Queen was getting herself in position for her next entrance.

"Why do you want her to?"

"My mother wanted her to. She's dead, you see."

The Fairy Queen gave Rachel a thinking look.

"Will you take a word of advice? Don't build your hopes too high. It's hard enough for those who want to succeed in the ballet world to get anywhere, so it's my bet that someone who would rather be one of Mrs. Wintle's Wonders wouldn't have a chance."

Rachel watched the Fairy Queen rise on her pointes, lift her arms and glide onto the stage. Puzzled, she stared at her. She danced so beautifully, yet she had left The Royal Ballet School because she knew she had not enough talent. "It's hard enough for those who want to succeed to get anywhere. It's my bet someone who would rather be a Wonder wouldn't have a chance!"

Rachel looked at Hilary. The Wonders, their golden buttercup-colored net skirts flying, were pirouetting around the Fairy Queen. Hilary unconsciously was holding out her pleated skirt and had one foot raised as if she was longing to join them. At that moment, though she did not know it, the first tiny seed of doubt about Hilary's future was sown in Rachel's mind.

The next day what Rachel most dreaded happened. The troupe of Wonders playing in *Mother Goose* on the outskirts of London had a case of chicken pox.

Actually, except for Dulcic's success it was an unlucky Christmas for Mrs. Wintle. In the north there was gastric flu, and five Wonders were hurried up there as replacements. In London one of the children dancing in *Alice in Wonderland* had handed around crab sandwiches which the matron said afterwards must have been "off." As a result, all the Wonders taking part in *Alice* were away for nearly a week. Not that they were ill the whole time, but, as the matron said: "They couldn't fancy dancing as oysters feeling queasy." Also, there were isolated illnesses in troupes all over the country: an appendix to come out here, tonsils there, and, it seemed to Mrs. Wintle, toothache everywhere. So the chicken pox was really the last straw.

The first case was reported on Rachel's twelfth birthday. She and Hilary had spent a lovely day with Uncle Tom, and came home after a visit to the circus to be met with the chicken pox news. It was bedtime anyway, so Uncle Tom did not notice that Rachel's spirits dropped as if down a well. But of course Hilary noticed. As soon as they were in their bedroom she said:

"I wouldn't fuss. The understudy will go on, and that girl Wendy in your group who has just got her license will be made understudy."

Rachel gloomily took off her coat.

"Don't try and cheer me up. I shouldn't wonder if half of them catch chicken pox. Then the barrel will have to be scraped, and I'll find myself a gosling."

"Perhaps all the *Mother Goose* Wonders have had chicken pox," Hilary suggested.

"They won't have. I feel it in my bones. And another thing I feel in my bones is that tomorrow there'll be an appointment made for me to be examined for my license."

Rachel's bones were quite right. Two days later she

was taken by Mrs. Storm to the County Hall to apply for a license. Before she was examined she had a faint hope the license might be refused, but it quickly died. The doctor who examined her said he wished all the children he saw were as healthy as she was. And the education man, knowing Mrs. Storm because she had brought Dulcie for examination, seemed to think that learning with her was proof a child's education was up to standard.

On her return to the school Rachel said sadly to Hilary:

"In front of you you see a licensed Wonder."

Rachel was right too about the chicken pox. Those *Mother Goose* Wonders who had not had it went down with it like ninepins, and only Wonders who had already had chicken pox could replace them. (Rachel and Hilary had shared chicken pox when they were in Hollywood.) The understudy took the place of the first case, and the child called Wendy became understudy. Then Wendy had to go on and a girl called Ruth understudied.

"The day Ruth goes on I must be understudy," said Rachel, "there's no one left who's had chicken pox in my group who knows the dances. Who'll understudy if I go on I can't imagine."

Two days later the blow fell.

"Another *Mother Goose* Wonder has chicken pox,

so you'll be understudy from tonight, Rachel," Pat said as if it were good news. "I'll run through the routines with you this morning."

Rachel had been sent before Christmas to watch a couple of rehearsals of *Mother Goose,* and, since the chicken pox started, she had been twice to the theater to watch the show. Both Pat and Ena had taught her the dances and the speciality in case she should be needed, so there was no real cause for her to be nervous. But she was.

"Although I'm only understudying," she said to Hilary as she put on her new Wonder's uniform, "I feel as I did before I was sick on the *Queen Elizabeth* coming back from Hollywood."

Hilary tried to answer her, but she laughed so much she choked.

"I don't know why," she gasped, "but somehow, got up as a Wonder, you look like a dog dressed up as a kitten."

Ordinarily, being an understudy meant just sitting about, but there was no sitting about for Rachel. There was still one Wonder in the troupe who had not had chicken pox, so Rachel knew that at any moment she might have to go on. And there was a great deal besides the routines to memorize.

"Please God," Rachel prayed fervently, "don't let

Gwen get chicken pox, because truly I'll make a terrible Wonder."

But her prayer was not answered. Three days after she had started understudying the telephone rang. It was Gwen's mother on the line.

"I'm sorry but Gwen's got it all right. You couldn't put a grain of rice between the spots."

"There's still hope," Rachel said to Hilary. "I'm so very bottom of the barrel that perhaps Aunt Cora will find somebody else and let me go on being understudy."

But the hope did not last long.

"You'll go on as of tonight," Pat said.

To Rachel's amazement she made no noticeable mistakes in *Mother Goose,* but she always felt she was going to and this, try as she would, made smiling very difficult.

"Funny kiddie, that last replacement," the stage manager said to the matron. "Doesn't look Mrs. Wintle's style somehow."

The matron made an agreeing face.

"She isn't. Dreams in the dressing room, or reads a book. I can't get her to play games. But the first chicken pox will be back next week, and then she can go back to being understudy."

Rachel was the first Wonder in the history of Mrs.

Wintle's school who was delighted to switch from being part of a troupe to being understudy. But her great day came when a second Wonder recovered from chicken pox and she was not even the understudy.

"I feel as if I'd been traveling for years through a coal-black tunnel," she told Mrs. Storm, "and now I'd come out into the sun."

21

MRS. STORM

Because Dulcie was such a success neither Rachel nor Hilary supposed Aunt Cora had time to think of anybody else. But they were wrong. Two days before the holidays ended Pursey, looking pink and flustered-hen-ish, came into the canteen.

"As soon as you've finished you're to go to your

Auntie, Rachel my lambkin. She's in the schoolroom."

Rachel, who had been feeling gay, at once felt scared and rather cold.

"What's she want me for? No one else is ill, are they?"

Pursey patted her shoulder.

"It's nothing to do with the theater. Now don't worry, it'll be all right." Then she hurried out of the room.

Rachel and Hilary looked at each other. Hilary said:

"It can't be as awful as Pursey made it sound."

Rachel put down the piece of bread and honey she had been going to eat.

"Whatever it is I better get it over, I couldn't eat any more with seeing her hanging over me."

Aunt Cora was sitting at the schoolroom table looking at both Rachel's and Dulcie's exercise books.

"Hullo, childie," she said, "sit down."

Rachel sat and tried to smile, but she did not feel at all like smiling, for Aunt Cora had never called her childie before and she thought the sudden use of so odd a word sinister. Even odder, Aunt Cora sounded as if she were trying to sound pleased to see her. What could she be going to say? Rachel soon found out.

"You appreciate, of course, what a success Dulcie

has made. I have put her in the hands of a theatrical agent. He expects a quite dazzling future for her."

The whole school expected a dazzling future for Dulcie, so Rachel was not surprised.

"I expect she will have."

"But of course," Aunt Cora went on, "she is only a little girl, and if, as the agent expects, she will be working in films and on television as well as in stage shows, we must not strain her too hard in other ways. Must we?"

Rachel tried to be helpful.

"Perhaps she could miss her first dancing lesson, and have breakfast in bed, and . . ."

Aunt Cora spoke sharply.

"Thank you. I am quite capable of arranging Dulcie's timetable. No, it is her lessons I'm thinking about. I hear from Mrs. Storm that you are advanced in your work, and indeed a study of your exercise books bears that out. . . ."

There was a pause, during which Rachel felt an answer was expected.

"I like lessons."

"I'm sure you do. That being so, I've decided that since I don't want Dulcie forced forward, nor of course you held back, you won't learn with Mrs. Storm this term . . ."

Rachel could not believe what she heard.

"Not learn with Mrs. Storm?"

Aunt Cora sounded cross.

"Don't repeat what I say in that stupid way. You would think I had told you the world was coming to an end, instead of merely informing you that in future you will attend the local school."

To Rachel a large part of her world was coming to an end. She had not realized until that minute how much she looked forward to Mrs. Storm's coming each morning. How exciting Mrs. Storm made the time before lessons began, giving words wings so that they flew round the schoolroom. Teaching her how to feel inside somebody else, whether it was Alice in Wonderland, a person in a play of Shakespeare's, someone in a fairy tale or in a modern play. Mrs. Storm did not know anything about proper dancing, but she was the only person except Hilary who could understand that everybody did not want to be a Wonder. Without meaning to Rachel found herself again repeating Aunt Cora's last words.

"The local school."

That made Aunt Cora really cross.

"My dear child, do try and show a grain of intelligence. Yes, the local school. I expect you will enjoy it, for several of my Wonders attend there when they are in London."

Rachel licked her lips.

"And Hilary?" The question came out haltingly.

"She will go on working with Mrs. Storm. I think it's more fun for Dulcie to have someone to work with."

That made Rachel angry.

"If I go to school then Hilary goes too. Why should she work with Dulcie . . ."

Rachel was going on to say "Just because you think it will be fun for Dulcie," but before she got the words out Aunt Cora stopped her, misunderstanding what she was thinking.

"Really, Rachel! I had hoped you had outgrown that jealous nonsense. The way you are always trying to stand in Hilary's light appalls me, and convinces me, if I needed convincing, that you are a bad influence in the schoolroom."

Rachel, to her disgust, started to cry, which hindered her saying what she wanted to say.

"I'm not jealous, and it's hateful of you to say I am . . . you've no right to separate us, we're sisters. . . ."

Aunt Cora thought Rachel was being maddening. She did her best to give her a nice home, and now, just because she had decided that she was rather too advanced in lessons to learn with Dulcie, she was making this scene. There was no thought of separating her and Hilary out of school hours, they would still share a bedroom, so why this fuss if it was not jealousy?

Of course the poor child had every reason to feel jealous, Hilary having not only better looks but talent as well.

"There's nothing to cry about, Rachel. Dry your eyes, and try and be sensible. Hilary is not your sister . . ."

Rachel struggled to find her handkerchief, which was lost in her knicker leg.

"She is . . . I mean, she's always been one, Daddy chose her . . . Mummie called her my sister . . ."

Aunt Cora looked at Rachel, and felt sorry for herself, for at that moment Rachel did not look like a niece who was a Wonder. Her face was greenish-yellow, her nose was pink, and, as always when she was trying not to cry, she was scowling.

"I'm not stopping you seeing her. You'll be together at meals, and you share a bedroom. Run along now and don't be a little goose."

Rachel ran. She went to her bedroom and lay on her bed and cried and cried and cried. "I'm not jealous," she sobbed, "I'm not, but I won't have her talking as if Hilary was Dulcie's slave. Oh goodness, how will I bear being alive with no Mrs. Storm, and probably a summer engagement as a Wonder?"

As soon as Rachel had left the room Aunt Cora wrote to Mrs. Storm and told her what was arranged. "I'll send this by hand," she thought as she sealed the letter. "Jenkins can drop it after he has taken Dulcie to the theater. I want the matter settled today."

Mrs. Storm was out when the letter arrived, but she found it when she came in to tea. An hour later Mr. Storm came home; he found Mrs. Storm raging up and down their sitting room like a lioness in a cage. She was so angry that it took him quite a long time to find out what the trouble was. But when he did he was very sensible.

"My dear girl, don't get all worked up about it. Go and see Mrs. Wintle, tell her what you think."

"When?" Mrs. Storm asked.

"Now," said Mr. Storm. "For I want a quiet evening, and I certainly won't get it until you've got the subject of Rachel's lessons off your chest."

Mrs. Wintle was also hoping for a quiet evening, but when Mrs. Storm knocked on her sitting room door there was a look in her eyes which showed her she was not going to have it. However, she pretended not to notice that anything was wrong.

"Hello, Mrs. Storm. How nice to see you. I hope you've had a good holiday?"

Mrs. Storm wasted no time.

"I've come in answer to your letter."

"Oh yes," said Mrs. Wintle, as if it were something of no importance, "about my plans for Rachel."

"I thought you'd better know right away that unless I teach Rachel I will not teach Dulcie or Hilary."

Mrs. Wintle could not believe her ears. Nobody for years had spoken to her like that.

"What do you mean?"

"What I say. I am a trained teacher, and I love my work. Rachel is an intelligent child, whom it is a pleasure to teach. Hilary is a lazy little thing, and Dulcie, though she's sharp enough, takes no interest in her lessons. I bother myself with Dulcie and Hilary because of the delight I get from teaching Rachel. Take her away and I should be wasting my talents."

"But I have said I wish . . ." Mrs. Wintle began.

But Mrs. Storm interrupted her.

"I'm afraid what you wish does not interest me. If I teach Rachel I will teach the other two, but if you send Rachel to a school I give you my notice. Perhaps you will let me know tomorrow what you decide. Good night."

It was Mrs. Wintle's turn to rage up and down like a lioness. Her first thought was to tell Mrs. Storm she could leave, that London was full of governesses all twice as clever as she was. Then she had wiser thoughts. Mrs. Storm was a very good teacher, and Mrs. Wintle knew it. The London County Council only granted licenses to children of school age provided their work was up to standard. Thanks to Mrs. Storm Dulcie's work was up to standard, but it had to stay up to standard. She had to go for examination every three months, and she was due for re-examination in a few weeks' time. Mrs. Storm had taken her for her first examination, and was supposed to be taking her to her next one. It was a bad moment for Dulcie to change governesses. Feeling very cross because she was not used to giving in, Mrs. Wintle picked up the telephone and rang Mrs. Storm's telephone number.

Before she went to bed Pursey very softly opened the door of Rachel and Hilary's room. Hilary was asleep, but Rachel, as Pursey was afraid she might be, was under the bedclothes crying. Pursey could not turn on the light because of Hilary, but she could see Rachel by the light in the hall, and a very woebegone, miserable, wet Rachel she looked. With a kind of mew she threw herself into Pursey's arms.

"I've held back crying all day because I didn't want Hilary to know. I said it was about lessons Aunt Cora wanted to see me and she said: 'Oh, was that all' and didn't ask any more. I couldn't tell her Aunt Cora thought I was jealous because she was to do lessons with Mrs. Storm and I wasn't, could I?"

Pursey hugged Rachel to her, rocking her to and fro.

"There, my lambkin, there. Of course you couldn't," she whispered, "and a good job you didn't.

You should have listened to old Pursey. She said it would be all right, didn't she? Well, it is."

Rachel, startled, raised a wet face.

"How?"

"Mrs. Storm came around, and talked to Mrs. W. I don't want to make you vain, dear, but it seems that if she can't teach you then she won't teach here at all."

Rachel was stunned.

"You don't mean she's dared to say that to Aunt Cora?"

"That's right, dearie. So that was that, and you'll be doing lessons as usual in the schoolroom the day after tomorrow."

It is difficult, when you have been drowning in misery, to reach happiness in one jump as it were, but Rachel managed it.

"Oh Pursey," she said as she wriggled down in bed, "how simply gorgeous! I couldn't have borne not seeing Mrs. Storm again."

Pursey kissed her.

"Of course you couldn't. But let this be a lesson to you not to get in a state too soon. Now off you go to sleep."

Rachel flung her arms around Pursey.

"Most gorgeous Pursey. You'll never, never know how much I love you."

22

NEWS FOR HILARY

Before lessons started on the first day of term Mrs.
Storm had a talk with Rachel.

"I can't understand why you have allowed your
aunt to think it was not that I would no longer be
teaching you that you minded, but that Hilary should
learn from me, and you shouldn't, which is nonsense."

Rachel did not like Mrs. Storm to think she had been stupid.

"She spoke as if Hilary was just a slave of Dulcie's."

"Which is impossible, and you know it. Hilary is not the type to be anyone's slave. You also know that she's quite capable of standing up for herself."

Rachel was not allowing that.

"Mummie always expected me to look after her. She said Hilary was irresponsible."

Mrs. Storm laughed.

"That's a long word. Do you know what it means?"

"Not being able to look after yourself."

Mrs. Storm nodded.

"More or less. Now can you look me in the eye and say that's true of Hilary today?"

Rachel tried to think clearly. It was true Hilary had managed in just under two years to be one of the best all-round dancers in Group one, which, if you wanted to be a Wonder, was pretty good going. Only Hilary ought not to want to be a Wonder . . .

"I think it's irresponsible to want to be good at the sort of dancing the Wonders do when you know it's not the sort of dancing you ought to be doing."

Mrs. Storm laid a hand on one of Rachel's.

"I think it's high time you accepted the fact that Hilary is much more competent to look after herself than you are." She saw Rachel was going to argue, so she went on quickly. "She is. I don't see Hilary meekly having her life upset without putting up a fight. I want you to think about that. It's no good your plotting and planning for Hilary, for I can promise you that, however fond of you she is, she will do what she wants to do and not what you want her to do."

The seed planted in Rachel's mind the day she had talked to the Fairy Queen cracked and put out a minute root. But Rachel did not know it.

"You don't understand . . . everybody at Folkestone knew she had to go to The Royal Ballet School. . ."

"I daresay, but you take my advice and think about yourself for a change."

Of course, in no time, without anyone knowing how they found out, all the Wonders were talking about the row between Mrs. Storm and Mrs. Wintle. The best story described Mrs. Wintle beating Mrs. Storm with an umbrella. Hilary did not meet many of her group at dancing classes as the pantomime season was not over, but a few came to the school and in a flash she had picked up a mixed collection of stories. She came to Rachel, her eyes dancing with excitement.

"That morning you went to see Aunt Cora and you said it was about lessons, was it to tell you that you were going to a boarding school?"

Rachel did not want to discuss that morning.

"Of course not. How could I learn to be a Wonder at a boarding school?"

"Well, did Mrs. Storm say that if she couldn't teach you she would rather lie down in the road and be run over by a bus than teach so awful a child as Dulcie? And did Aunt Cora beat her with her umbrella?"

That made Rachel laugh.

"Of course Aunt Cora didn't. And Mrs. Storm wouldn't say anything about lying down in the road."

"You are the most miserable describer," Hilary groaned. "Everybody knows something exciting happened. What was it? Don't be mean, all the Wonders depend on me to find out."

"Aunt Cora talked about a day school. . ."

"The one near here where some of the Wonders go?"

"I think that was it."

"Well, why aren't we going?" Hilary asked.

"You never were, it was only me."

Hilary could not believe her ears.

"Rachel Lennox, do you mean to say your Aunt Cora was planning to send you to school, which would be fun, and leave me slaving with Dulcie?"

Hilary's way of thinking was so different from her own that Rachel found it difficult to explain.

"I didn't think it sounded fun."

Hilary was disgusted.

210

"You wouldn't. And you never told me. You were just letting me be sacrificed as a burnt offering without raising a finger to save me? What a sister!"

"I was angry at her separating us, but mostly I suppose I was minding not learning any more with Mrs. Storm. Anyway it hasn't happened."

Hilary had been practicing the splits while she talked. Now she stood up and came close to Rachel and put on a persuasive voice.

"There was a row, wasn't there? And Mrs. Storm did call Dulcie 'your revolting daughter.' That did happen, didn't it?"

Rachel felt quite apologetic at spoiling Hilary's story.

"I'm certain it didn't. What Mrs. Storm did say was that I was the only one who liked lessons, so she wanted to go on teaching me and . . ."

Hilary put her fingers in her ears.

"Don't tell me, I don't want to hear. It's the most gorgeous story, and you're making it duller every minute. I'd rather believe the Wonders."

Dulcie's pantomime finished but she did not stop working. Her agent, who was called Mr. Al Purk, got her several little engagements. She made a film for television, advertising soap, in which she had to dance. She appeared in a television variety show and in a children's television panel game.

Luck came to the whole house out of Dulcie's television engagements, for because Mrs. Wintle thought everybody ought to watch her daughter, she put a television set in the canteen. Before it came the only television set had been in her sitting room, which meant no one looked at it except the Wintles. And, as Hilary said, you had to be pretty desperate to sit watching a programme with Aunt Cora and Dulcie.

Now that there was a television set in the canteen Pursey, Yolanta, Wanda and anybody who had stayed on late would sit glued to the set, eating sweets or cakes made by Wanda. And very cozy and happy they all were. When Dulcie appeared, even advertising soap, it made Wanda's and Yolanta's day. They were so proud their eyebrows went up, the corners of their mouths, their hands, even their feet, while they crooned "She is yooist the most beautiful liddle girl."

Dulcie on television puzzled Hilary.

"As a matter of fact," she said to Rachel, "she does look all right, doesn't she? But it's odd that she looks nice. The Wonders say their mothers suppose they're jealous when they say what they think of her. People say the television screen can't lie, but it lies all right about Dulcie. You could say all sorts of things about her but nobody could say she was nice."

It certainly was very hard for Rachel, Hilary, or for Mrs. Storm to think of Dulcie as nice that term.

She had always been pleased with herself, but that term she was conceited beyond bearing. She truly thought Rachel and Hilary lucky to be allowed to learn with her, and Mrs. Storm lucky to be allowed to teach her.

"Why is it," Mrs. Storm asked Pursey, "when the whole school is, I hear, quacking about my argument with Mrs. Wintle, that Dulcie, who would be the better for knowing what happened, clearly knows nothing about it?"

"Ah well," said Pursey in her cozy voice, "she wouldn't. She never did mix with the Wonders, and since she's been Red Riding Hood and on television I'm afraid she's Miss High-and-Mighty."

"I'll say she is," Mrs. Storm agreed. "Honestly, Pursey, if it wasn't for Rachel I'd leave tomorrow."

Pursey shook her head.

"Don't ever think that way, dear. I don't like to see Dulcie as she is any more than you do, but it's Dulcie I'm sorry for. Pride always has a fall, and when Miss High-and-Mighty has hers a terrible fall it will be."

"I hope my tender heart will break when that happens," said Mrs. Storm, "but I doubt it."

Hilary had a gorgeous twelfth birthday. Uncle Tom had absolutely refused to say what was going to happen, and so had Pursey, so she and Rachel had not even known what sort of clothes to wear. But they had soon found out, for Pursey, when she brought them a birthday breakfast in bed, brought amongst Hilary's parcels a picture puzzle drawn by Uncle Tom of how they were spending the day. The first drawing had shown Hilary and Rachel dressed in their everyday clothes at the Zoo. Then there was a picture of them resting, with dreams of the animals they had seen chasing each other round the ceiling. Then a funny one of them changing into best dresses, and then one of them sitting watching what turned out to be The Royal Ballet dancing *The Sleeping Princess.*

Inside her Hilary had been disappointed when she had discovered Uncle Tom was taking her and Rachel to *The Sleeping Princess.* She thought he was doing it to get her to like ballet to please Rachel. But once the curtain was up she had forgotten all about being disappointed and instead had been carried along as if on wings by the lovely dancing and the fairy story.

But of course to Hilary the best thing about her birthday was that she was of an age to be a Wonder. And though she would not have admitted it even to Rachel she was a bit nervous when Mrs. Storm took her to County Hall for her license.

But it was all right. Hilary was never sure if it was that the man who examined her had faith in Mrs. Storm, or whether by luck she could answer the questions she was asked, but she was granted her license.

Mrs. Storm must have guessed Hilary had not felt too happy for, as they came out of County Hall, she said something she had never thought of saying to Dulcie, or even to Rachel.

"I think this calls for an ice."

Just before Easter Dulcie got a really grand stage engagement. A big new musical was about to go into rehearsal and there was a part for a child in it. Dozens of little girls were auditioned, but Dulcie was engaged.

"And that's only a beginning, Mrs. W.," said Mr. Al Purk, rubbing his hands together in a pleased way. "There's interest in the little lady in the film world. She'll have a contract for pictures before the year's out, you'll see."

"Well, that settles her for the summer," said Hilary. "Now everybody's got to hold their thumbs for me. What I want is a long engagement by the sea."

But there was no engagement by the sea for Hilary. The day after Dulcie signed her contract Hilary was bustled into her uniform and little-girl frock and taken in a taxi by Mrs. Wintle herself to see Dulcie's manager. She came back to the school looking, for her, really crushed.

"Imagine, girls," she told her group. "Talk about a living death, no one could guess what horror is happening to me this summer. I've got to understudy dear, dear little Dulcie."

23

REHEARSAL TROUBLE

Dulcie's musical was a story about Austria. There were three sisters in it, and Dulcie played the youngest. Her part was small but what Mr. Al Purk described as showy. It was for convenience that Hilary had been picked as Dulcie's understudy.

"Have you got a clever child suitable for the understudy?" Dulcie's manager had asked. "She can share Dulcie's dressing room, be looked after by the same woman and, of course, do lessons with Dulcie."

The obvious answer was Hilary. Mrs. Wintle was not altogether pleased at having to choose her. She would have preferred a less attractive and clever child as the understudy. It was not likely Dulcie would ever be off, but if it were to happen a rather plain but adequate substitute was the answer, a child who would make the management sigh for the return of brilliant little Dulcie. Hilary was attractive, Mrs. Wintle had to admit, though of course nothing like as pretty as Dulcie, and she was a good dancer, though without Dulcie's all-round talent and polish. But Mrs. Wintle had to weigh convenience against a possible rival for Dulcie, and convenience won.

The beginning of Dulcie's rehearsals happened during the Easter holidays. Hilary, who of course had to watch rehearsals, told Rachel about the play.

"It's in a place called the Tyrol, and Dulcie's one of the daughters of the man who keeps the inn. The story's soppy, all about love, but Dulcie's father and a little American man are gorgeously funny, and there is some terrific dancing."

"Ballet?"

Hilary grinned.

"It's no good hoping, they don't do that in the

217

Tyrol. Some of it's that slap-your-tail-and-stamp sort of dancing," Hilary broke off to imitate Austrian folk dancing, "but mostly it's a very grand kind of musical comedy."

"What does Dulcie do?"

"That Friedl that she is, is an awfully silly girl, and she has some awfully silly things to do. She skips—well, it's a skipping dance really, with a rope of flowers."

"I can see Dulcie doing that," said Rachel.

Hilary sounded gloomy.

"You will. As a matter of fact she does it very well, if you like that sort of thing, but I don't."

"What else does she do?"

"She sings a song in a swing, she's not so good at that, and she's going to have lots of little bits in the grown-up dancers' routines. They're not fixed yet, but they'll be good, I think."

"Why do you say Friedl's silly?"

Hilary thought.

"She hasn't got much to say, and everything that she does say is silly, but I think Dulcie makes her sillier than she is. You know the way Dulcie says things."

When the Easter holidays finished it was decided that while the play was in rehearsal lessons for both Dulcie and Hilary should take place in the theater wardrobe. That of course meant Rachel did her lessons there too. It also meant that Rachel and Mrs. Storm watched rehearsals, which was how they came to be in the theater on the day Dulcie met trouble.

It was a week before the first dress rehearsal, when the American who had written the words of the musical arrived at the theater. He sat in the stalls near where Mrs. Storm was sitting between Rachel and Hilary. Hilary, who always knew everything, knew who the man was, and to their great embarrassment, for they were afraid he would hear, told Rachel and Mrs. Storm in a piercing whisper.

"That's Fred K. Scholtz. He wrote the words, not the music."

If Fred K. Scholtz heard Hilary's whisper he made no sign, but sat absorbed in what was happening on the stage, now and again making notes on a writing pad. But when the act was over he was a quite different person. He shot out of his seat, through the stage box to the pass door and onto the stage. All the cast were called back to hear what he had to say.

The play had first been produced in New York so Mr. Fred K. Scholtz knew what it should be like, and though on the whole he was pleased there were things he did not like; one of them was the way Dulcie said her lines.

"Where's the little girl who plays Friedl?"

Dulcie, very sure of herself, skipped forward.

"Here I am."

Mr. Fred K. Scholtz looked at her in a kind but puzzled way.

"You do that skipping rope dance beautifully, better than little Sonia who played Friedl on Broadway, but your lines! You know, I don't think you have your mind on what you are saying."

Dulcie was astounded. Praise, praise, praise was all she had heard. Mrs. Storm, Pat and Ena scolded her sometimes, but who cared for them? But it could not happen in a theater. She gave Mr. Fred K. Scholtz a very proud look.

"Of course I have."

Mr. Fred K. Scholtz shook his head.

"If you have it does not sound like it. See that you watch yourself in the second act."

"Good," Hilary whispered. "Perhaps she'll be less cocky now."

Mrs. Storm might not like Dulcie but she was not allowing that.

"I hope you listened to what Mr. Scholtz said, for you never have your mind on what you are saying."

Hilary grinned at Mrs. Storm.

"But Miss Hilary Lennox doesn't want to act parts, and Miss Dulcie Wintle does."

In the second act Dulcie had her song in the swing.

It was a simple, almost nursery rhyme sort of song. It did not suit Dulcie, who was not at her best doing things simply. The way she sang it so upset Mr. Fred K. Scholtz that he stopped the rehearsal.

He jumped out of his seat and ran to the orchestra pit.

"No no no! little girl, you want to sing these words as if you were singing a doll to sleep."

Dulcie got out of the swing and came to the footlights. She shielded her eyes with one hand so that she could see Mr. Fred K. Scholtz.

"I sang it as I've been told to sing it."

This was not quite true, for at every rehearsal Dulcie had been told not to dramatize the song, but all the same the producer thought it was rather hard on somebody of twelve to be picked on before the whole cast. Very nicely he came onto the stage and put an arm around Dulcie.

"I expect I'm to blame. Shall we pass it for now, and I'll take Dulcie through it with you afterwards?"

But Mr. Fred K. Scholtz wanted immediate action. Little Sonia had been a great success in that song on Broadway, and he wanted to be sure Dulcie had the same success in London.

"We'll work at it later if you like, but I'm sure this little lady can put the number over if she tries, can't you, my dear?"

Dulcie was furious but at the same time a tiny bit scared. It was so odd to be criticized. She was wonderful, everybody knew she was wonderful. Why couldn't Mr. Scholtz see how clever she was?

Mr. Scholtz was thinking of nothing but the good of his play.

"Now hop back into that swing and imagine you're all alone singing to a baby doll."

To be angry and scared at the same time is not the best way to feel while you are singing to a baby doll. Dulcie sang the song worse than she had the first time, and she knew it, which was so humiliating to her pride that she burst into tears.

Nobody liked that, for however Dulcie said her lines or sang that song she was a very pretty and talented child. The producer thought the kindest thing would be to give her a little rest. He looked into the theater.

"Is the governess there?"

"Yes," said Mrs. Storm.

"Take Dulcie up to her room, will you? We'll manage without her until after the lunch break. The understudy can take her place this morning."

This was the last thing that Dulcie wanted, and her tears turned almost into hysterics. The producer could feel the whole cast was distressed, so as Mrs. Storm led Dulcie away he said cheerfully:

Rehearsal Trouble

"Come on, everybody. Dulcie will be all right this afternoon. Now, where's that understudy?"

Thanks to Mrs. Storm's efforts Hilary knew her lines. She also, from having watched the rehearsals, knew every entrance and exit, and she had of course learned the dances. But she had never thought about Friedl, the sort of girl she was meant to be or how she would play the part if ever she had to play it. So when she suddenly, to her great disgust, found she had to rehearse in place of Dulcie, instead of trying to feel like Friedl she gave an imitation of Dulcie being Friedl.

At first everybody thought what an excellent understudy Hilary was, but towards the end of the act there was an amusing modern dance by the chorus in which Dulcie took part, and in this Hilary let herself go. It was intended that Dulcie should give a slightly exaggerated imitation of a rather showing-off child. Hilary, enjoying herself at last, gave a really funny caricature of Dulcie's performance. It was so funny that she had everybody who was watching laughing.

"That kid's a scream," the stage manager whispered to the producer.

The producer nodded.

"She's got nothing like Dulcie's polish, but we're quite safe if she has to go on."

Of course Dulcie knew that Hilary was thought a good understudy, for that is the sort of thing it is impossible to keep secret in a theater. But until Mr. Fred K. Scholtz came to rehearsal, she had supposed that she was so clever and so pretty that nobody could replace her. She did not really worry about Hilary, who, she was certain, had nowhere near as much talent as she had, but she was not taking any risks, so she got Mrs. Storm alone.

"Will you help me with my song in the swing, and with my lines?"

Mrs. Storm, for the first time since she had been Dulcie's governess, admired the girl.

"Of course, dear, I'll be pleased to." She would have liked to have added: "And you're a sensible girl to bury your pride and admit you need help," but she was too wise to say so.

Partly thanks to Mrs. Storm working with Dulcie, and partly because, for the first time, Dulcie had to believe she was not quite perfect, she had no further trouble with her part. In fact, though the musical did not get very good notices, Dulcie did. This of course made her forget the trouble at rehearsal, and become apparently her own bouncy conceited self. But it was only apparently, for right inside her where nobody else knew about it was a nervous Dulcie. This Dulcie had learned something every actress has to learn sooner or later, which is that she is not indispensable. And Dulcie did not like it one little bit.

24

HILARY FIGHTS

Just after the musical began its run Rachel, with others of her group, had to attend an audition for a touring revue. Children attending auditions had to assemble in the front hall to be looked over by Pursey, and perhaps afterwards by Mrs. Wintle, before they left the school.

Rachel felt dreadfully self-conscious in her little-girl frock, for she knew it did not suit her. She was the last in a row of twenty-one Wonders lined up for inspection. Hilary, feeling much as a hospital nurse must feel when presenting to the doctor a patient she personally has prepared for an operation, hovered in the background.

When Rachel and Hilary woke up that morning the position of elder and younger sister had been reversed, for it was Hilary who took charge.

"I've been thinking about your hair," she said to Rachel. "Those plaits suit you, but the uniform hat looks awful on top of them."

"Shall I wear them unpinned?" Rachel suggested. "I could get some blue ribbon from Pursey to tie on the ends of my plaits."

Hilary looked at Rachel with the face some mothers wear when one of their children is being exceptionally stupid.

"No Wonder has its hair plaited for an audition. Even you must know that, Rachel. Almost all are specially curled, and don't forget, more often than not your Aunt Cora comes to wish the kiddiewinks good luck before they go, so you must look right."

Rachel had never bothered to watch what happened before auditions. Now, seeing Hilary's shocked eyes, she realized that she should have done so.

"I'll wear it loose if you say so."

"Loose, and curled," said Hilary firmly. "Pursey has a curling iron. I'll get her to do it."

So Rachel's hair was loose and curled. The style was not becoming to her serious, high-cheekboned face, but, as Hilary observed, it did make her look at least from the back very much like the other girls of her group. Thanks to Hilary, Rachel ought to have looked like the others from the front too, for her summer uniform coat was hanging on her left arm, and open at her feet were her attaché case with the right shoes in it and, of course, a brush and comb. She was wearing her clean, little-girl frock, and her socks were spotless. Yet somehow from the front she looked all wrong. No matter how often Hilary had twitched at her hat to pull it to the proper Wonder angle it had skidded on Rachel's fuzzed hair and sat on the top of her head. There was not a thing wrong with her little-girl frock, but on Rachel it looked ridiculous.

"Perhaps she's standing wrong," thought Hilary worriedly. "None of the rest of us make those frocks look odd, but she does."

Mrs. Wintle did inspect the Wonders that afternoon, and behind her, every inch a star, pranced Dulcie. To do her justice Mrs. Wintle did not want to pick on Rachel. In fact when she first arrived in the hall, to her relief a quick glance in Rachel's direction had shown her a most correct-looking Wonder. But when she reached Rachel she felt irritated, as she had so often felt before when looking at her. All the other twenty Wonders were excited about the audition, and looked it. Rachel, though bored at having to go to an audition, had hidden it. But when her Aunt Cora appeared she felt scared, and went stiff all over. In fact, by the time Aunt Cora was standing in front of her Rachel looked like a dummy in a shop window. Perhaps, as it was the first time Rachel had been to an audition, Mrs. Wintle would have managed to hold back her irritation and said nothing, but Dulcie made that impossible. She put both hands over her mouth and giggled in a hissing way. Then she gurgled:

"Sorry, Rachel, but you do look funny in your uniform frock."

Hilary, afterwards cross-examined by the Wonders, never knew if she decided to do what she did or whether it happened before she had time to think. At any rate, in a flash she had rushed around to Dulcie and had given her cheek a very noisy slap.

Mrs. Wintle waited until the Wonders had left for their audition. Then she said in a voice which sounded like chips being hacked off a block of ice:

"I will see you now, Hilary, in my sitting room."

Any other child in the school would have been

cowed, but not Hilary. She knew quite well that she ought not to have hit Dulcie, and that keeping her temper but telling Dulcie exactly what she thought of her rudeness would have been more effective. But she was not repentant, for she was glad she had stood up for Rachel.

Mrs. Wintle sat at her desk and told Hilary to face her.

"Aren't you ashamed of yourself?"

"No."

That answer was a surprise, and for a moment left Mrs. Wintle wondering what to say next.

"Why aren't you?"

"If anyone's ashamed it ought to be Dulcie," Hilary explained. "She's got everything, and Rachel's got nothing, so it was awfully mean to laugh at her."

Mrs. Wintle was silenced. Could that be true? It was certainly true that Dulcie had everything, and that poor plain untalented Rachel had nothing. At last she said:

"Perhaps it was not kind of Dulcie, but you should not have hit her, should you?"

"No," Hilary agreed, "I shouldn't—though, mind you, a few hits won't do Dulcie any harm."

Mrs. Wintle's voice sounded more like chips off a block of ice than ever.

"She's a wonderfully talented child. I'm afraid you are jealous of her."

That made Hilary laugh.

"Not me. I would simply hate to be her."

"Why?"

"I don't like hard work. I hope she'll never be off, for I don't want to go on for her. All I want is to be an ordinary Wonder."

Mrs. Wintle disliked lack of keenness in her pupils.

"Nonsense. All my Wonders are ambitious. I can understand your dread of going on for Dulcie, after the success she has made. What I can't understand is why you should wish to defend Rachel. She doesn't stand up for you."

"I don't need standing up for," Hilary explained, "but if I did she would."

"I don't want to come between you and Rachel," Mrs. Wintle said untruthfully, "but I think you ought to know that Rachel, far from standing up for you, has on many occasions shown me that she is jealous of you."

Hilary thought that a most idiotic remark.

"Of me! What would she be jealous of me for?"

"Your talents. You are one of the more promising children I am training, and she, poor child, one of the least . . ."

"Me being promising wouldn't make Rachel jealous."

"Then there are your looks. You are, I hope, going to be nice looking, whereas poor Rachel . . ."

Hilary seldom saw the Rachel that Mrs. Wintle almost always saw.

"I think Rachel looks gorgeous. Madame Raine, who taught me dancing at Folkestone, said it ought to have been her who danced, not me, as she had classic beauty."

Mrs. Wintle simply did not believe that.

"Nonsense. You and Rachel are two silly little girls. One would think from the way you behave that I was trying to stand in your way, instead of doing everything I can to insure that you both have a successful future."

Hilary thought that another silly remark.

"Rachel won't be a successful Wonder. She hates being one."

Mrs. Wintle did not want to hear Hilary's views on Rachel. Rachel was a Wonder, and all Wonders enjoyed their work. So she turned back to the afternoon's crime.

"You must, of course, apologize to Dulcie."

"I won't," said Hilary, "unless she apologizes to Rachel."

Mrs. Wintle saw that getting apologies would take a long time. She had meant to give Hilary a punishment as well as making her apologize, but now she pretended she had planned on one or the other.

"Very well then, I must punish you. You will go to bed immediately after supper on Sunday. In other words, no television."

Hilary looked Mrs. Wintle squarely in the eyes.

"Is Dulcie being punished too? She started it."

"I shall speak to Dulcie, but you are old enough to understand that she's a very exceptional little girl, highly sensitive, and cannot be treated as an ordinary child such as yourself."

"I know that's what you think," Hilary agreed, "but if I was her mother I'd punish her. It was mean of her to laugh at Rachel, and you can't say it wasn't."

Hilary liked having the last word, so on that she marched out of the room and shut the door.

Mrs. Wintle, as she usually did when anything went wrong, visited the wardrobe to talk things over with Pursey. Pursey had broken off work to have a cup of tea, and now she poured one out for Mrs. Wintle.

"I thought you'd be along, Mrs. W. It's this business of Hilary slapping Dulcie, I suppose."

Mrs. Wintle sat on a wardrobe basket.

"Yes. It was very wrong of her. It might have upset Dulcie before tonight's show."

Pursey stirred her tea before she answered.

"Very fond of each other, Rachel and Hilary are. No wonder, I suppose, left on their own, like."

"That's no reason why Hilary should hit poor little Dulcie."

Pursey did not answer that directly.

"If Hilary has been to question me once about this audition she's been fifty times. Was Rachel's little-girl frock—that's what she calls the audition dresses—exactly like all the others? Was her summer coat the right length? Yesterday I found her going through one of Rachel's drawers to be sure she had a clean pair of socks . . ."

"I daresay," Mrs. Wintle interrupted, "but none of this excuses her hitting Dulcie. And whatever trouble you and Hilary may have taken, the fact is Rachel does look a figure of fun in her uniform."

Pursey went on in her cozy voice, just as if Mrs. Wintle had not spoken.

"Then this morning ever so early Hilary brings Rachel in here and asks will I curl her hair. Well, I know it doesn't suit Rachel to have her hair curled, but . . ."

Mrs. Wintle sniffed.

"Nothing suits that child."

"That's a matter of opinion," said Pursey, "but I couldn't put Hilary off curls for Rachel. 'I want her,' she said, 'to look as if more trouble had been taken over her than over any of the others.' Rachel herself didn't care how she looked, but . . ."

Mrs. Wintle put down her cup.

"That I can well believe."

"But," Pursey went on quietly, "Hilary did, so I curled Rachel's hair. Hilary's smart and I don't suppose she thought Rachel looked right in the frock. But with all the trouble she'd gone to to see that Rachel looked as near right as possible, it must have been cruel when Dulcie laughed and, in front of all the Wonders, said Rachel looked funny."

"Well, she did look funny."

Pursey poured more tea into Mrs. Wintle's cup.

"I daresay, but Dulcie should have been better behaved than to have said so."

"What d'you want me to do?" said Mrs. Wintle crossly. "I suppose you're not going to say Hilary was right to hit her."

Pursey shook her head.

"No. Hitting, biting, scratching and such I've never stood for in my nurseries. But if it was my school, with feelings running high as they will, whatever punishment I gave Hilary I would give Dulcie."

Mrs. Wintle could not punish her little star, so instead that evening she said to her:

"I know Mum's girlie could not help laughing at

Rachel, for she does look terrible in her uniform frock. But some people think you meant to be unkind. Would you be a good generous girl and run in during Group three's tap class tomorrow and give Rachel a kiss and say you're sorry. It would be a kind thing to do, especially as she was not even considered at the audition."

It took time to persuade Dulcie, but she did not want all the Wonders saying she had behaved badly, so in the end she agreed. The next afternoon a goggle-eyed Group three watched Dulcie very prettily kiss an awkward embarrassed Rachel and heard her say: "I'm sorry I said you looked funny."

Though the incident seemed to end there it did not quite. Before it happened, Rachel, to Mrs. Wintle, was one sort of person and Hilary quite another. But from now onward they became fixed together in her mind like William and Mary. In fact, from that day onward she frequently spoke of them as one person. "Now about Rachelanhilary." And the word she used to describe both was "tiresome."

25

LITTLE-GIRL FROCK

Uncle Tom was fond of drawing Rachel's head. Perhaps because he had drawn it so often he was one of
the first to notice that she was wearing more and more
often a hang-dog expression. He did not say anything
until he was sure it was not a passing mood, then one
Sunday when she was in his studio he asked:

"What's the matter, old lady?"

Rachel was sitting on the floor sorting out the contents of what had once been a paintbox but which had become a junk box.

"Nothing."

"Nonsense," said Uncle Tom. "Come here." Rachel got up off the floor and came to his side. "Look at this," Uncle Tom said and drew Rachel's mouth when it smiled. "And now at this." He drew her mouth pulled down at the corners. "This is the mouth I am seeing every day now. The smiling one is the mouth I used to see. So it's no good saying nothing is the matter."

Rachel hesitated, then she blurted out:

"I'm feeling inferior."

Uncle Tom thought people talked about private things best when they were not being stared at, so he started drawing again.

"Why?"

"It sounds silly, because you know I don't want to be a Wonder, but you can't think what it does to you when you go to audition after audition and the most unlikely Wonders are picked, but never you."

Uncle Tom tried to understand.

"I suppose it hurts, but seeing how much you dislike being a Wonder isn't it a relief to find you don't have to be one?"

Rachel nodded. Then she went on:

"That's absolutely true, and most of me knows it's silly to mind. But there's a bit of me that feels the way a puppy in a shop window must feel when all the other puppies are bought but never him."

Uncle Tom stopped painting and gave his whole attention to Rachel.

"Let's get to the bottom of this. Why are you never chosen? Can't you manage the dancing?"

"Of course I can, every routine and all the audition songs. I'm not a good dancer, but I'm as good as most of Group three. I think truly it's my audition frock."

"What's the matter with it?"

"Nothing. I mean Hilary looks awfully nice in hers but I look terrible in mine and I know it."

"Doesn't it fit?"

Rachel sighed at his ignorance.

"Of course it fits. Our audition dresses have to fit, one inch above the knee and all that. No, it's me. I wasn't born for frills. If you could see me in it you'd understand what I mean."

Uncle Tom had to accept that however strange he might find it Rachel really was minding wearing this particular frock.

"Well, let me see it. Go and put it on."

Uncle Tom believed Rachel would be beautiful

when she grew up. Already, to him, she was interesting looking, with her expressive dark eyes and sensitive, high-cheekboned face. But hers was a face that easily looked unhappy, and that obviously, he supposed, was the expression that for some reason managers were seeing. It was probably, he guessed, Rachel's expression and not the frock that kept managers from engaging her as a Wonder. But when Rachel came in dressed for an audition he knew his guess had been wrong, and he used an expression he used only when he was thunderstruck.

"Let me swim with my Aunt Fanny up the Suez Canal!"

Rachel had decided it would be best that Uncle Tom should see her exactly as she looked at an audition. So she had not only changed into her little-girl frock but had unplaited her hair and tied it on either side with small blue bows.

Rachel had exaggerated when she said that none of the other Wonders found anything wrong with the audition dresses. They had been designed to make the children look younger than they were, so it was not a kind dress to many of them. They were made of seersucker, very full and without a waistline, with frills on the shoulders and around the bottom. To dress Rachel in such a frock was like putting a cloth over a lamp, for it dimmed her until there was no Rachel left. It took away a sort of dignity which was part of her, and made her instead look silly.

"My poor child," Uncle Tom said, "that certainly is a disaster of a dress."

Rachel looked at him searchingly to be sure he was speaking the truth.

"Could I be engaged as a Wonder wearing it?"

Uncle Tom slowly shook his head.

"Not unless every other available Wonder had spots and a squint."

Rachel felt as if she had been carrying something heavy on her back, and it had fallen off.

"Goodness, I'm glad you said that! It truly is the frock and not me?" Uncle Tom nodded. "Knowing that for certain, I shan't be humiliated however many auditions I go to without being engaged."

Uncle Tom had held back laughing, but now he let it out in a great roar, and as he laughed he hugged Rachel to him.

"My poor Rachel," he gasped, "if you could see yourself—what a frock! It is the most horrible dress I ever saw." Then he took a deep breath and got control of his laughter. "I'm sorry to laugh, but you do look a comic. But I tell you what we'll do. I'll design some frocks for you and we'll get Pursey to make them. Then when you come back from an audition you can put on one of my frocks to take away the taste of that blue horror. Now run along and change before I'm sick."

In early July Dulcie's musical ended its run. Mrs. Wintle was not pleased, for she wanted any show Dulcie was in to be a success. But, as she told Pursey, coming off when it did had its advantages.

"Dulcie needs a holiday. I think this year, after a quick tour of the Wonders, her father and I will take her abroad. If you can bear it you might stay on in the holiday camp with Rachelanhilary."

Pursey secretly thought there was nothing she would enjoy more than some Wintle-less weeks in a holiday camp. She could see herself watching whatever was going on while she had a cozy gossip with one of the matrons. As for Rachel and Hilary, bless their hearts, of course she could bear having them, and if they did not enjoy themselves it would not be old Pursey's fault. But for everybody's sake it was not a good idea to look too pleased, so she only said in her cozy voice:

"That's the idea, you go off somewhere. Nothing like abroad for a real change, they say. You leave Rachel and Hilary to me; they'll be all right."

It turned out to be a glorious holiday for everybody. The Wintles went to Spain, where Dulcie watched and learned Spanish dancing, while Uncle

Tom wandered off alone blissfully painting. At the holiday camp the weather was perfect. Pursey spent hours talking happily to the matrons. Hilary lived on the sands, superbly happy playing and working with the Wonders.

"See if you can walk into the sea on your hands."

"Look, I can do this backwards."

Rachel, free for the first time in nearly two and a half years from Aunt Cora's sharp eyes and despising face, enjoyed every second. Each day she bathed with Hilary and the Wonders, but when they started acrobatics she wandered off either to lie behind a rock near by and read undisturbed or to walk along the sands dreamily, looking into the sea pools and watching the sea birds. When she was out of hearing of everybody she would work at Mrs. Storm's homework, filling her lungs full of air while she told the sea gulls to "Make me a willow cabin at your gate," or that "The quality of mercy is not strain'd."

Then it was the autumn term again, and to everybody's amazement, especially Mrs. Wintle's, Mr. Al Purk's, and, of course, Dulcie's own, the little star was out of work. There was not a nibble. No television, no film, no theater. Then one day, just as the auditions for the Christmas shows were about to start, the telephone rang. It was Dulcie's producer on the line.

"I'm doing a new children's show this Christmas, Mrs. Wintle."

Mrs. Wintle tried not to sound eager.

"And you want Dulcie?"

"No. The child I have my eye on is your niece, Hilary."

26

ROSE-COLORED GLASSES

The play in which Hilary was to dance was not the
sort of play in which the Wonders ordinarily appeared. It was an unusual children's play called *Rose-
colored Glasses,* written by a well-known poet. Hilary
did not care who had written *Rose-colored Glasses* for

she did not want a part in any play. She told the producer so when she was taken to see him.

"What d'you want me for? I won't be any good."

The producer was thoroughly amused.

"I'm sorry if I've inconvenienced you. But there's a comic robin in this new children's play which I thought would suit you."

"Has he anything to say?"

"No, it's all mime with a little dancing."

Hilary gave in grudgingly.

"Well, I suppose I'll have to be him."

The producer laughed.

"Don't you want to? Most children would jump at the chance. I thought I was doing you a good turn."

"Well, you aren't. All I want to be is just an ordinary Wonder, and look what happens to me. My first engagement is to understudy Dulcie, which nobody could like, and now I've got to be a robin. Wouldn't you rather have somebody else? There are heaps of Wonders who'd be better than me."

The producer gave Hilary's hair an affectionate rub.

"You're a card. But no, thank you. I'm sticking to you."

Mrs. Storm had read in the papers about *Rose-colored Glasses* and was delighted that Hilary was to dance in it.

"I hope we can see it. It ought to be a lovely production."

"I hope, as she's a robin, Hilary will do real proper dancing," Rachel said. "I expect she will. You couldn't really do acrobatics or tap as a bird, could you? They don't."

Mrs. Storm had no views about the sort of dancing robins would do, so Rachel daydreamed of Hilary with fluttering wings dancing on her pointes. She went further, she imagined someone from The Royal Ballet School seeing her and insisting that she leave Mrs. Wintle and go there to learn. So it was a nasty shock when Hilary came back from her first rehearsal and she heard what dancing she really had to do.

It was a Saturday afternoon and classes were over, so the canteen was full of Wonders drinking tea and eating buns. Hilary sat on a table and told everybody, including Rachel, about her rehearsal.

"The story's about some children who come from where the sun always shines to live in London. They loathe it because they think it's always wet and gray. Actually they're rather soppy types."

Questions rang out.

"How many children?"

"Who plays them?"

"What school trains them?"

"They seem like amateurs to me," Hilary said.

"There are two boys and one girl. I think they're relations of the author's, or something like that."

"What happens next, Hilary?" one of the Wonders asked.

"A spirit thing turns up. I heard someone say he was going to be dressed like a beefeater, but I shouldn't think he is, because he has wings, which beefeaters couldn't have. Anyway, he tells the children that he will lend them magic spectacles so they can see properly."

"Where do you come in?" Rachel asked.

"When the spirit thing has lent the children invisible spectacles, which are pink, he sends for me to be their guide and take them back into history times."

"But you dance, don't you?" said Rachel.

Hilary climbed off the table.

"If you call it dancing. Clear a space and I'll show you."

Hilary, of course, could not help making fun of herself being a robin, but even allowing for the fact that she was exaggerating it was clear to Rachel that there were no fluttering wings and no dancing on her pointes.

"It's a pity," Rachel thought, "but one good thing, Hilary doesn't really want to be the robin. It would be much worse if she liked doing that sort of dancing." But even as she was thinking this a little nagging voice was whispering: "Hilary doesn't want to be the robin because she's lazy, it's not because she isn't dancing real ballet. And you know it." Rachel could not silence the little nagging voice, for the seed planted by the Fairy Queen had taken firm root. Besides, deep inside her, she knew the voice was speaking the truth.

As Christmas came nearer troupe after troupe of Wonders left London for provincial theaters, and most of those remaining in London were called to rehearsals. The school could not help gloating.

"Dulcie's almost the only child not working, except of course Rachel," the Wonders whispered to one another. "I bet she feels awful with Hilary having a part while she's out of work."

Dulcie did not mind Hilary's having a part as much as the Wonders supposed, for she had heard what the part of the robin was like, and knew it would not have suited her. But after Mr. Al Purk's promises, and all that her mother had said about future contracts, she certainly was disappointed that no work was offered her.

Mrs. Storm felt a kind of admiration for Dulcie at that time. Any other conceited child who had been praised and made a fuss of would, she thought, have felt a bit subdued when no engagement turned up after all the talk about a glittering future. But not Dulcie. Whatever she felt inside, there was not a sign of it outside her, for she was just as bouncy and grand as if she were still playing a lead in the musical.

Rose-colored Glasses opened for matinées only, three days before Christmas. Because it had been her intention that Hilary should start her career that Christmas as an ordinary Wonder, Mrs. Wintle had to pretend that being the robin in *Rose-colored Glasses* was not important. And from a money viewpoint it was not important, for Hilary earned very little more than she had earned as Dulcie's understudy. But from the critics' point of view *Rose-colored Glasses* was an important play, partly because of the author and partly because it was a long time since there had been a good new children's entertainment. Because she had let it be understood that she did not think anything of Hilary's part Mrs. Wintle did not go to the first performance.

"Will you take Rachel to see that little play Hilary's in?" she said to Mrs. Storm. "It's my busiest time, as you know. I'll pop in and see it one day after Christmas."

It was Mrs. Wintle's busiest time, though she could have managed the matinée if she had wanted to, and it was also everybody else's busy time. Pat and Ena were rushing from theater to theater, and Wanda and Yolanta were serving meals at all hours. Dulcie, though bursting to know how good Hilary was, had no intention of admitting it, so instead of going to watch her performance she went with her mother to a dress rehearsal of *Cinderella*. So it happened that Mrs. Storm and Rachel were the only two people from the school in the theater at the first performance. And because their interest was in the acting and neither knew anything about the sort of modern dancing Hilary had to do they did not realize how good she was. After the performance there was a tea party at the author's house for the children in the show, so Hilary did not go back to the school with Rachel.

Rachel was having tea in the canteen when Mrs. Wintle and Dulcie came home from *Cinderella*.

"How did Hilary get on?" Aunt Cora called out.

Rachel jumped nervously and wondered what was the right answer. It would take too long to explain that it was mostly an acting play and Hilary had nothing to say.

"All right, I think. People clapped."

"Mostly kids in the audience, I suppose," said Dulcie.

Rachel had spent the two intervals discussing the play and the acting with Mrs. Storm, and had not noticed who was in the theater.

"Grownups too, I think," she said doubtfully.

Mrs. Wintle carried her tray of tea to a table as far from Rachel as possible. Aggravating child, why did she have to look as if she were about to be beaten every time she spoke to her?

"Oh well," she said, biting back her thoughts, "I'm glad Hilary didn't disgrace the school even if she didn't shine. Come and have your tea, Dulcie, Mum's girl must be tired."

The next day the papers were full of *Rose-colored Glasses,* and nearly all of them had something nice to say about Hilary as the cheeky little robin. Some of the reviewers wrote just as good things about her as the best things they had written about Dulcie.

Mrs. Wintle read the reviews with mounting anger. It was nonsense, Hilary was not as clever as that. It was probably a showy little part. She hated Hilary's reviews so much she had to be angry with somebody. The person she chose was Rachel. It was intolerable, she told herself, how Rachel behaved to Hilary. Why couldn't she be honest and admit Hilary was a success. "She was all right, I think," and now look at the reviews.

Neither Rachel nor Hilary had seen the papers, and over their bacon and eggs they were not discussing *Rose-colored Glasses,* but Christmas presents. They were so deep in their talk they did not see Aunt Cora until she was standing by their table.

"Congratulations, Hilary," Aunt Cora said in a very unpleased voice. "It's lucky I take all the papers for if I had depended on Rachel's report you might have been a failure."

Hilary knew Rachel and Mrs. Storm had enjoyed the play, but she also realized why Rachel had not given a good description of her part.

"Rachel doesn't know about dancing. She liked the play."

Aunt Cora would have enjoyed shaking Hilary as well as Rachel.

"It's heart-breaking, Rachel. You'll be thirteen next month, and have been trained by me for three years . . ."

Hilary interrupted her.

"Three years in March."

"Don't quibble," said Aunt Cora. "And not only can you not get even understudy work to the Group three Wonders but you can't report to me correctly on how Hilary danced."

With twinkling eyes, Hilary watched Aunt Cora leave the room. Then she helped herself to another piece of toast.

"I wonder what that was all about. I shouldn't think I could have got good enough notices for her to be jealous for Dulcie. But we'd better buy all the papers and find out."

27

THE STUDIO

Because *Rose-colored Glasses* attracted attention all through its run photographs of the cast appeared in lots of papers and magazines, Hilary's amongst them. As well, she was interviewed in a programme on television called *Personalities on Parade*, and in this she was considered one of the television hits of the week.

"Are you nervous?" the interviewer asked her.

"Not a bit," Hilary replied truthfully. "But I'm in a hurry, because there's a thriller I want to get home in time to see."

When asked if she was enjoying playing the robin, she said:

"Not really. Quite truthfully I don't want solo parts. What I want is to dance in a troupe."

Asked if some day she would like to be a star, she said, with horror in her voice:

"Not likely. I hate work."

Dulcie found Hilary's success hard to bear. It made it worse that Hilary took everything for granted, and was not particularly interested. Dulcie was not exactly jealous of her, for she had been to see *Rose-colored Glasses* and, though she thought Hilary was good, she could see that her success was more because the part of the robin suited her than because of what she did with it. But she minded dreadfully that it was Hilary the school talked about and not her. She was much too proud to say so, but she dreaded going backstage with her mother to visit the Wonders, for she thought she knew what they were saying about her. But she kept her dread to herself and, if anything, looked prouder than usual. Certainly she sounded grander, for after her mother's "Well done, chicka-biddies. We were proud of them, weren't we, Dulcie?"

she looked round with a kind smile to answer: "I thought you did awfully well."

If Dulcie could have known what the Wonders were really saying she would have minded visiting them even more than she did.

"Poor old Dulcie-Pulsie." "Pretty sickening for her not working, and Hilary being such a success." "Can't help being sorry for her."

Even though she did not know the Wonders were pitying her, night after night Dulcie would roll over on her face and mutter into her pillow. "It isn't fair. I'm clever, and I'm going to have a great future. Everybody knows I am. Why doesn't Al Purk get me some work? Why haven't I got a film contract? He said I would have one. . . ."

Rachel had to work for three weeks in *Aladdin*. This year it was ordinary colds that put the Wonders to bed. She started as understudy, but after two nights she had to go on.

"It's worse than last year," she told Hilary gloomily, "for in Aladdin's cave we're all jewels, and have steps to do alone. I'm a little diamond, and I look terrible, for the dress doesn't fit me anywhere."

For convenience, while the matinées of *Rose-colored Glasses* lasted, Hilary did her lessons with the other children in the cast in the theater wardrobe. She was delighted, for the governess at the theater was not half as strict as Mrs. Storm. The arrangement did not please anybody else.

"Just because Hilary is not your pupil for a few weeks that doesn't mean I want Dulcie forced up to Rachel's standard," Mrs. Wintle told Mrs. Storm. "She will be taking extra outside elocution classes, and that with her dancing is more than enough."

"I wish your play would come off," Rachel told Hilary. "I hate lessons with Dulcie only. I feel she's waiting to pounce on me."

"I miss Hilary," Mrs. Storm told Mr. Storm. "She's a lazy little thing, but she finds Dulcie's airs and graces funny, whereas Rachel is at her worst when she is alone with her. There's never an open quarrel but I'm always afraid Dulcie will start saying something about Hilary and then there will be."

Quite likely the quarrel Mrs. Storm dreaded would have happened had not some exciting news for Dulcie put everything else out of her mind. It started with a small column in a Sunday paper.

"In some schoolroom a dark-haired child is working, whose name in a few months' time will be known all over the world. The reason is that a film is to be made of that best-selling novel *Flotsam*. My tip to the director is to remember a small girl who made a big hit last year in a short-lived musical."

Neither Mrs. Wintle nor Dulcie could bear to wait

for Mr. Al Purk's office to open on Monday; when it did there was good news.

"It's all lined up," said Mr. Al Purk. "As I told them last week, they won't have far to look for a dark-haired child. They'll see Dulcie on Thursday."

"Are they seeing only Dulcie?"

"Maybe a few others. But I've a hunch Tony Bing, who's directing, knows who he wants, and my guess is it's little Dulcie."

To Dulcie the news that she probably was going to star in a film was like the difference between a fine day in summer and a cold wct one in winter. Her mother was as pleased and excited as she was.

"Only three days," she told Mrs. Storm, "and such a lot to do. She must have a new frock, and I must have her hair done. And I want you to read *Flotsam* to her so that she gets an idea of the part."

Although it was not exactly lessons, *Flotsam* was a well-written book, so Mrs. Storm stretched a point and allowed reading it to count as literature. It was a long book to get through, even with skipping, so she read it to Dulcie and Rachel during breaks in the afternoons.

The heroine of the book was a child called Vera. At the beginning of the story she lived in an orphanage. Nobody knew anything about her, as when she was a baby she had been the only person rescued

from a ship which had been torpedoed off Singapore
in the last war. The sailors who rescued her had christened the baby Vera. When the story proper started
Vera was thirteen, a queer lonely little girl. Then her
life changed. A rich old couple whose son had lived
in Singapore, where he had been killed, learned that
he had been married, and that there had been a baby.
It was possible that the baby was Vera. So they took
Vera to live with them on trial to see if she was the
sort of child their son might have had. To Vera a real
home and living in the country was paradise after the
orphanage, but she was so different, except in color-
ing, from the son the old people remembered, that
they decided she was not their grandchild. What the
old people had to learn was that it is the way a child
is brought up, the qualities with which it is born,
rather than who its parents were, that form a character. Just at the end of the book they discovered that
they loved Vera for herself, so it did not matter if she
was their grandchild or not.

"Well, Dulcie," said Mrs. Storm as she closed the
book, "do you think you could act Vera?"

Dulcie was sure she could act any part.

"Of course I could."

Mrs. Storm could not imagine Dulcie being good
as Vera, but she could see why she might get the part.
She was dark, which Vera had to be, and she had the

sort of face which looked extra pretty on a film or television screen. Besides which, acting in a film was quite different from acting in a play: the scenes were shot one at a time. Probably a good coach could make Dulcie say her lines in the way the director wanted.

On Thursday a very excited Dulcie went with her mother to her interview. But a more subdued Dulcie came back, so subdued that at first the rumor raced round the school that she had not got the part of Vera. But later Pursey heard the true story. Mrs. Wintle told it to her.

"I feel sure Dulcie will get the part. It was clear that Mr. Bing, who is directing the picture, was very taken with her. But he has another thirty girls to see, imagine! I call it a waste of time. He is fixing film tests for the probables next week, which of course means a test for Dulcie."

Sure enough, the next week Dulcie went for her film test. This time she came back in wild spirits, so the gossip was she had almost got the part of Vera.

"It's not definite," Mrs. Wintle told Pursey, "but Al Purk is pretty hopeful. He's even gone so far as to discuss money. She'll start at a hundred pounds a week for this film, but he expects it will lead to a long contract at more money."

Pursey did not believe in counting chickens before they were hatched.

"I wouldn't get too set on the film, dear. If Dulcie is meant to play it she'll play it, and if she isn't something else will turn up."

Mrs. Wintle looked at Pursey with despair mixed with affection.

"You're a silly old goose. This is Dulcie's great chance. A part like this won't turn up again. She'll get it. I know she'll get it. I see her name in enormous electric lights."

Pursey saw she could not stop Mrs. Wintle counting unhatched chickens, so she said:

"Well, I hope there's news one way or the other soon. It isn't good for you or Dulcie either getting yourselves into such a state."

When the next news came Mrs. Wintle was away. There had been a letter from the holiday camp manager, who was planning to use more Wonders that year, asking her to come north to see him. Mrs. Wintle had not wanted to go, but Al Purk, when asked on the telephone, said he thought it would be all right.

"You can trust me, Mrs. W. I've got my spies out, and they tell me the studio are still looking at the tests, but that our little lady heads the list. I don't think we'll hear anything for another day or so."

But Mrs. Wintle's train had only just left the station when the telephone bell rang at the school.

"Would Mrs. Wintle bring Dulcie to the studio that

afternoon? Mr. Bing wanted to have a talk with her."

Pat took the message and knew that with Mrs. Wintle away only one person could decide who should take Dulcie to the studio, and that was Dulcie's father. A few minutes later Uncle Tom walked into the schoolroom.

"Sorry to interrupt, Mrs. Storm, but they want Dulcie at the studio this afternoon. As my wife's away will you take her?" Then he thought about Rachel. "You'd better go along too, old lady."

Dulcie was so excited that she danced around the room.

"Imagine if I telephone Mum tonight to say I've got the film contract! Won't she be pleased? May I go and tell Pursey to press my new frock?"

Mrs. Storm corrected her.

"You may go and ask Pursey if she will do it."

"What ought I to wear, do you suppose?" Rachel asked Mrs. Storm while Dulcie was out of the room.

"Is a studio a place where I'll have to wear my Wonder's uniform?"

Mrs. Storm had no idea what Mrs. Wintle would have answered to that, but she knew her own feelings.

"For goodness sake don't. Wear what you like. Nobody's going to look at you."

What Rachel liked was an orange woolen frock, one of the dresses which Uncle Tom had designed for her. Over it she put on a brown coat. She did not wear a hat. Under her arm she carried her favorite book, *The Wind in the Willows,* which she knew from experience was wonderful for making time disappear. However long she had to wait at the studio the time would slide away while she lived on the river bank with Moley, Ratty and Toad.

"Very nice too," said Mrs. Storm approvingly when she saw Rachel. "Those colors suit you."

Mr. Bing had seen four girls that day before he saw Dulcie. They were the final choice out of the hundred odd he had first interviewed. Dulcie, as Al Purk had said, headed the list. So that the children being interviewed had room to move about Mr. Bing was seeing them not in his office but on the studio floor. With him were his secretary, Miss Orton, and his assistant director, Mr. Brown. As they waited they looked through the still photographs that had been taken of Dulcie.

"It's certainly a lovely little face," said Mr. Brown.

Mr. Bing sighed in a worried way.

"But is it the face Vera would have had? That's what I ask myself."

Miss Orton picked up another photograph.

"To me it is. But I'm not sure of her voice."

"Neither am I," Mr. Bing agreed. "If I could make

up my mind about that I'd tell Al Purk to go ahead with the contract."

"That new coach, Mrs. Robinson, isn't worried," Mr. Brown reminded him. "She says the child's clever, and she's sure she can be taught to do anything you want."

Mr. Bing tossed the photographs on the table.

"I don't want a taught child, I want one that can feel. But I suppose it's no good expecting a miracle. Pop along, Brown, and tell Dulcie we're ready to see her."

Rachel and Mrs. Storm sat down on two chairs a scene shifter pointed out to them. They were near enough to hear what went on but not near enough to be in the way. Watching Dulcie was so interesting that Rachel forgot *The Wind in the Willows* and felt as if she were in a theater watching a play.

Dulcie was told to show Mr. Bing how she would act Vera the first time she met her possible grandparents. There was a door on the set, and over and over again Dulcie came through it, saying: "I'm Vera. Vera Valiant they call me. It was the name of the ship that rescued me." Sometimes Dulcie did something, or said her lines as Mr. Bing liked, but more often she was not right.

"No, my dear," he said. "You're not a successful

child actress now, you're a lonely little creature from an orphanage."

Then Mr. Bing changed the scene. There was a place in the book where Vera first discovered a bird's nest. To help, a tree with a nest in it had been put up. That should have been an easy scene for Dulcie, but unfortunately for her she did not find birds' nests interesting, and she did not sound as if she did. She only had to say: "A nest! With eggs in it!" But though she tried hard she evidently did not say the words quite as Mr. Bing wanted them said.

The last scene Mr. Bing wanted was a sad one. It was the moment when Vera learned the old people had decided she was not their grandchild, and must go back to the orphanage. In the book Vera said good-by to the house and garden, and that was what Mr. Bing wanted Dulcie to pretend she was doing.

"I want you to make up lines. Just good-by will do. Pretend you've got favorite trees and plants which you won't see again."

Dulcie was, Rachel thought, rather good in that scene, for she did seem to be sad, and she did seem to be looking at plants and trees. But still she had not given Mr. Bing what he wanted. He jumped out of his chair and ran to her.

"No, my dear, no. You're doing it all too prettily. This matters to you, you are feeling as Eve must have felt when she was turned out of the Garden of Eden. Now, let me show you. Give me your hand." He turned, and as he did so he saw Rachel. He dropped Dulcie's hand and came over to her.

"Where have you sprung from? Brown, Miss Orton, come here. If this child can act our search is over. This is the face I've been looking for."

28

THE END OF THE STORY

Rachel thought how lucky it was that she was wearing
Uncle Tom's frock. How awful if she had been dressed
as a Wonder, for she was told to take off her coat and
play the scenes Dulcie had just acted. Imagine being
Vera in her little-girl frock!

Standing outside the property door, through which

she had to enter, Rachel knew exactly how Vera would feel at that moment. "Like me," she thought, "waiting to go in to Aunt Cora's sitting room. Only it will be worse for Vera because I had a home of my own once, and she never had one."

In such silence that if a mouse had dropped a whisker it would have been heard Rachel opened the door and, looking directly at Mr. Bing but seeing Aunt Cora, said in a nervous whisper: "I'm Vera. Vera Valiant they call me. It was the name of the ship that rescued me."

As she finished speaking Mr. Bing said in an awed voice:

"And I said I could not expect a miracle. I only hope this child really exists, and that I'm not dreaming."

Everything was not settled that day, for there had to be a film test, but three days later Al Purk, very scared, brought Mrs. Wintle Rachel's contract.

"Wonderful terms, Mrs. W.," he said. "They'll pay Mrs. Storm's salary, and there'll be transport, and . . ."

Mrs. Wintle's voice might have been spending a week in a refrigerator.

"Her uncle will sign. He is Rachel's legal guardian. Her affairs have nothing to do with me."

Rachel's taking the part of Vera from under Dulcie's nose caused a sensation in the school, but nobody dared speak about it except in a whisper. Mrs. Wintle was in such a bad mood no one even looked at her unless she spoke first, and then they scurried out of her sight as quickly as they could. Many of the Wonders, and Pat and Ena, would have liked to say something kind to Dulcie, but they did not dare, for she had cried off and on since she had left the studio, and they were afraid anything they said might make her cry again. For, as Pursey had always prophesied, Miss High-and-Mighty had fallen, and no fall could have been harder. It was bad enough at the last moment not getting the film contract, but that Rachel, the despised Rachel, should get it in her place was beyond bearing.

Mrs. Wintle, in the bitterness of her disappointment, had to blame somebody, so she turned on Mrs. Storm. It had been deliberate deceit coaching Rachel behind her back, making an actress of her without saying a word to anyone. What did Mrs. Storm think she, Mrs. Wintle, looked like in Mr. Bing's eyes? Already he was asking why he had to find Rachel by accident when she knew he was looking for a dark child who could act. Why had not Rachel been brought to him in the first place as a possible? Why had nobody remembered that her father was a film

star, and that his daughter might have inherited his
talent?

Mrs. Storm knew that had Mrs. Wintle known that
Rachel could act, she would never have let her near
the film studio, while there was a chance of Dulcie
getting the contract. But she did not say so. "Poor
woman," she thought, "she has deserved a knock, but
now that she's got it I can't help feeling sorry for
her."

For some days after her contract was signed Rachel's
mind was in such a whirl she could not think clearly.
Each afternoon, as soon as she finished lessons, a
studio car fetched her, and a chaperone chosen by the
studio took her to have her frocks for the film fitted,
and to be photographed. One afternoon she was taken
to meet the important people who ran the film company that was making *Flotsam*.

"I can't believe it's me," she told Uncle Tom. "I
know just how odd Alice felt in *Alice in Wonderland*.
You can't think how queer it is to be the last scraping
in the bottom of the barrel one minute and Vera in
Flotsam the next."

But at last it was Sunday, with no lessons and no
visit to the studio, so Rachel had time to think. Lying
in bed on Sunday night, looking at the hump which
she knew to be Hilary asleep, she felt as if all the day's

thinking had come to a point like a newly sharpened pencil.

"I am going to make a lot of money. I can't have it to spend now, but Uncle Tom would arrange that I could borrow some of it. Hilary needn't wait until I'm fifteen, she could start training now, right away. But will she? How can I make her see that she ought to?"

Having a question turning over and over in your mind is not the best way to go to sleep. The clock struck ten, then eleven, then twelve. "Perhaps," thought Rachel, "if I moved about a bit I'd get sleepy." Very quietly, so as not to wake Hilary, she got out of bed and went over to the window. Gently she pulled back the curtains and looked out.

There was an almost full moon, and by its light the dreary street looked nearly romantic. The shabby houses opposite were black majestic shadows, which the squeezed-together shops seemed to look up to admiringly. A black cat streaked up the road, and it was watching him that made Rachel strain sideways so that she lost her balance. To save herself she caught at the edge of the dressing table and sent everything flying with a clatter onto the floor.

Hilary sat up in bed yawning.

"What on earth are you doing? It must be the middle of the night."

Rachel apologized and explained.

Hilary got out of bed and rummaged in one of the dressing table drawers.

"Perhaps something to eat will make you sleepy. I've got two chocolates left from that box I was given after the last performance of *Rose-colored Glasses*." She found the chocolates and joined Rachel at the window. "Would you like a violet on the top of yours or a walnut?"

Rachel took the walnut.

"It was thinking that was keeping me awake."

"What about?" asked Hilary indistinctly because of her mouth being full.

"You, I mean . . ."

"Don't tell me," said Hilary. "I was wondering when that was coming. Now that you're going to earn a lot of money you want me to try and get into The Royal Ballet School."

"Will you?" Rachel asked.

"I won't go near the place. First, because if I was auditioned they wouldn't take me, and secondly, because I don't want to."

"But don't you remember Mummie saying about your lessons with Madame Raine: 'That's one thing we shall never give up . . .'?"

" 'Rachel and I are expecting to be kept in luxury by our star ballerina,' " Hilary added. "Of course

I remember. But she only thought I ought to dance because my mother did. She wouldn't really have cared if, I didn't. I knew your film contract would make you think about my dancing, so I asked Uncle Tom."

"What did he say?"

"He said he remembered your mother, and his guess was that if she were here she would want us to do the things we do best."

It was difficult to let her dream for Hilary go, but Rachel could feel she was going to.

"I wish I knew that was true."

Hilary skipped across the room and got back into bed.

"Stop worrying. Of course it's true. Think of all the mothers there must be fussing over their children tonight . . ."

"You mean Aunt Cora's fussing over Dulcie? In a way I feel mean about her."

"Don't," said Hilary. "Dulcie's not an acting person, and she wouldn't have been good as Vera. But she'll have that glittering future Mr. Al Purk talks about. Your Aunt Cora has always said she would see Dulcie's name in big electric lights, and I bet she will. They may not be as big as yours but she'll be a star, you'll see."

"I'd much rather know you would be one."

Hilary wriggled cozily down into bed.

"You'll never see that. I daresay I'll have to do some more dancing parts, like the robin, and I might dance for a bit in a chorus when I'm grown up, but I won't do it for long."

"What will you do instead?"

"I'm going to marry young and have lots and lots of children. I can see me with them."

"I can't see you liking looking after lots of children."

"I shan't have to," said Hilary in a very sure voice. "Pursey will come and live with me and look after them."

Rachel dropped her dream. She had done all she could. Hilary could not be turned into a ballerina.

"It seems a waste of talent," she said regretfully.

Hilary tucked her blankets firmly around herself.

"Waste nothing. What's nicer than babies? Now stop fussing and go to sleep. As orphans go we aren't doing too badly."

The MS READ-a-thon needs young readers!

Boys and girls between 6 and 14 can join the MS READ-a-thon and help find a cure for Multiple Sclerosis by reading books. And they get two rewards — the enjoyment of reading, and the great feeling that comes from helping others.

Parents and educators: For complete information call your local MS chapter, or call toll-free (800) 243-6000. Or mail the coupon below.

Kids can help, too!

Mail to:
National Multiple Sclerosis Society
205 East 42nd Street
New York, N.Y. 10017

I would like more information about the MS READ-a-thon and how it can work in my area.

MS
Mystery
Sleuth

Name_____
(please print)

Address_____

City_____State_____Zip_____

Organization_____

MS-10/77